The Dogf

written by Gerard Mac

Illustrations by Jan Szymczuk

First published in Great Britain 2013 by Laffin Books and Powdene Publicity Ltd,
Unit 17, Quay Level, St. Peter's Wharf, Newcastle upon Tyne, NE6 1TZ

A catalogue record for this book is available from the British Library.
ISBN: 978-0-9926969-0-0
Printed by Penny Print, Tyne and Wear

Gerard Mac, an author and journalist, wrote thrillers and historical novels (published by Robert Hale) before he wrote *The Dogfather,* his only children's book. Although his relationship with Northumberland was relatively short he grew very fond of the area. He first visited the village of Warkworth in 2006 when he was deposited at the Warkworth House Hotel by relatives and asked to check out a house they were thinking of buying. Spending an evening alone there, he received a warm welcome in the nearby Black Bull before he went for a walk, falling asleep on a bench along The Butts, and waking very late. He was clearly relaxed.

In the following years he became a regular visitor to Warkworth, holidaying there three or four times a year in the summer and during the festive period. In 2009 he bought a Blenheim Cavalier King Charles spaniel puppy, named Ria, for his granddaughter. Inspired by the interaction between the dogs they met, Gerard enjoyed taking Ria around their favourite village haunts after a long walk on the beach.

Sadly Gerard died in 2011, but Ria can often be found in the Warkworth House Hotel or the Black Bull where she unwinds after a long walk and enjoys a biscuit and a big fuss.

The Dogfather was Gerard's way of saying thank you to Warkworth, for the happy times he spent there.

Enjoy....

JIMMY, a Border Collie - Manchester Terrier Cross

RIA, a Blenheim Cavalier King Charles Spaniel

THE DOGFATHER,
'Don' Schnauzer

THE PROFESSOR,
a Bloodhound

PADDY, an Irish Setter

LULU, a French Poodle

ROCKY & RAMBO,
rottweilers

MAX, a German
Shepherd

RHAVI, an
Afghan Hound

RINGO, a
Beagle

CHALKIE, a
West Highland
Terrier

Two of the Pit Bull
PUPPIES

CHAPTER ONE

She had never spoken to him before. She had always walked past with her head held high, her nose in the air and her tail wagging as if to say, 'I'm too good for the likes of you.'

She was one of those King Charles spaniels, a Blenheim no less, with a coat of lovely brown and white patches, long floppy ears and the most beautiful eyes he had ever seen. But he didn't like her much. She was too full of herself. In fact, she thought she was the bee's knees, whatever that means.

Now she surprised him by stopping in her tracks, slowly turning and coming back. 'I say, you're Jimmy aren't you?' she said, in her posh King Charles' voice. 'You belong to that street gang.'

'Do I?' Jimmy said, looking round to make sure she was talking to him.

'There's no use denying it. Everyone *knows* you do. You're one of the leaders.'

'Am I?' he said.

'Well I've decided,' she announced. 'I've made up my mind.'

'About what?' he asked tolerantly.

'I want to see your real leader. What do they call him?'

'The Dogfather?'

'Yes,' she said, with an air of contempt. 'I suppose you get that from that stupid film about gangs in America.'

'Great film,' Jimmy said. 'Have you seen it?'

'Of course not,' she said. 'My people watch ballet and opera. They don't watch violent rubbish.'

She was being snooty again.

'Is that a fact?' he said. 'Well, if you want to see the Dogfather you are going to have to show a little respect. Or maybe more. A *lot* of respect.'

'Can he really fix things?' she asked.

'Depends,' Jimmy said.

Her voice had softened. She was not being snooty any more and he was falling under her spell.

'Well, I would be very grateful,' she said coyly, 'if you would arrange for me to meet him, Jimmy.'

'I'll see what I can do,' he said.

She turned to leave.

'Wait,' he said. 'I don't know *your* name.'

'It's Ria,'

'Ria?'

'My folks liked Maria in *The Sound of Music* so they called me Ria,' she told him and this time she did leave. She turned and went on her way, her head held high, her tail wagging. But this time she looked back and gave him her most captivating smile.

The Sound of Music, he thought. That was all about nuns and hills and stuff. Not his kind of thing. But there was another film with a Maria in it. Two gangs. Jets and Sharks. He liked that one best and he went on his way singing, 'Maria! I once knew a [illegible] called Maria!'

He knew he ought to have asked her what she wanted Don Schnauzer to fix. She might be asking the impossible or it might be something or nothing. But he wanted to see her again and he wasted no time in arranging a meeting.

Jimmy's heart was dancing that morning with the feeling that life was beginning all over again as winter crept silently away, banished by the coming of spring.

He lived in a lovely little village in Northumberland called Warkwood, with a village green and a village store where anything from pots and pans to pensions and postage stamps could be had.

There was just one main road that went right through the village and too often cars came through going far too fast to somewhere else. But on Bank Holidays and throughout the summer most of the cars stopped and people spent the day in the tea rooms and gift shops and some people even went for a walk by the river or to the beach or up to the castle to gaze at the ruins.

High up on a hillside was a medieval castle where knights and even kings once trod its green swards. Below the village was the river endlessly flowing to and from the great North Sea and less than a mile away was a glorious stretch of uncluttered beach.

It was a place where visitors came out of curiosity and many returned year after year. And, of course, those who actually lived in Warkwood knew everyone else who lived there and everyone else who lived there knew them. It was the same with the dogs. The dogs all knew each other and almost all of them were members of the gang.

A large black cat was squatting lazily on a garden wall as Jimmy went by. Jimmy gave it a friendly nod and the cat's green eyes flickered in response. He was on nodding terms with several of the local cats, but cats seemed to keep themselves to themselves. They didn't seem to get together like the dogs. But then, he thought, cats seemed to stay out pretty late. Maybe their gangs met by moonlight. But he didn't really know and it was none of his business anyway.

Don Schnauzer was sitting in a copse in the field at the back of Park Row. Most of the gang lived around here and it was easy to summon them when there was something to do or to discuss. There was a Beagle called Ringo and he had this bark they could all recognise. At a signal from The Don, Ringo would go to the edge of the copse, bark three times, count up to five then bark again and soon they would all come running.

Don Schnauzer, with his long-haired chin and veiled eyes, looked at Jimmy sadly. Would the boy never learn? Jimmy had obviously been charmed by this little madam and he didn't even know what it was she wanted.

The Professor, a bloodhound with long sagging cheeks and large heavy rings under his eyes, as if he had been up all night reading, was by The Don's side. He shook his head slowly. Don Schnauzer consulted The Professor on most things. Or, at least, he discussed matters with The Professor when there was a job to be done. But the final decision was always The Don's and his alone.

Seated on The Don's other side was Chalkie, a West Highland Terrier. He was a little fellow, not much good in a fight and he couldn't run to save his life. But he was always nice, not like some of those snappy little terriers, and he had this lovely Scot's accent. Everybody loved him and it didn't matter that he couldn't fight. Don Schnauzer didn't approve of dogs fighting among themselves. That was for humans and other animals who didn't know any better.

'Och, Jimmy, ye should have asked the lassie what she wanted,' Chalkie said with a smile. 'Ye ken that.'

Jimmy nodded sadly and was about to turn away when The Don said, 'Tell her ten o'clock tomorrow morning. I'll see her at ten.'

The next morning the sun was shining, but it was not the settled summer sunshine we sometimes get in June. It was the thin April sun that often carries a hint of rain on the way. Even so, word had gone round and the next morning they were all there at nine thirty, all except Paddy. Most of them knew this snooty King Charles [illegible] or, at least, they knew who she was and they were curious to know what she wanted.

'She's probably a nice lass,' Chalkie said to no one in particular.

The Don, flanked as usual by The Professor on one side and Chalkie on the other, presided over the meeting.

Max, the German shepherd, was there. He was getting on a bit now – he was at least fourteen years old – and he was always lying down as though he was half asleep. But he had been quite a dog in his day. When he was young he was in the Army. He did a dangerous job in those days, sniffing out landmines and bombs and stuff like that, and when he retired the Regiment awarded him a medal. He always wore it on a ribbon around his neck when he marched with his owner on Armistice Day.

Then he was in the police force, sniffing out drugs and things at the airport. It wasn't fair really. He would often get almost on board the aircraft, sniffing at passengers as they came off, yet he never got to fly. Anyway, he liked his last job, working as a guide dog, best.

He used to take care of this blind man and it seemed to the others that all he had to do was stroll around the village and down to the pub, making sure his man stopped at the roadside and didn't walk into walls and things. But he always said there was much more to it than that.

Nowadays he lived with an elderly gentleman who couldn't see very well and as Max couldn't see very well either, they took care of each other. The old man slept a lot during the day so Max had plenty of time to himself and he enjoyed being in the gang.

He was easily the biggest of the members but he didn't want to be boss or anything. He was just a big amiable lazy old dog these days. But he was still a good dog to have around in the event of trouble.

Sitting up, alongside where Max lay stretched out, was Rhavi, an Afghan hound. He had bright eyes and he looked as though he was ready for anything. He was a really reliable member of the gang. Rhavi lived at the village store.

The village store stayed open quite late, later than most of the other shops in the village, and he worked a lot of hours, mostly in the evenings. He was not allowed in the store, not officially anyway. His job was to sit in the doorway and sometimes growl and look scary if any yobs thought they could terrorise Ali, the store owner.

Once when Ringo the Beagle overheard some of them plotting to run through the store, stealing things as they went, he told Rhavi and Rhavi told the Dogfather. When the louts turned up, just before their bus was due to take them back to where they came from, they got quite a shock. The whole gang was there to chase them off.

But it wasn't necessary. Max told the assembled gang, 'Hang on, fellas. You can leave this to me.'

He stepped forward, put his head down, narrowed his eyes and let out a low terrifying growl. None of them missed their bus.

All the gang liked Ali the storekeeper. He was a nice man and he was very kind. Sometimes, when the weather was bad or it was raining really hard, he would let them hold their meetings under the carport at the back of the store. Most people with carports would shout at them and shoo them off. But not Ali.

Ali would greet them with, 'Hi there, my four-legged friends. Come in out of the rain, have we?' And sometimes he would give them biscuits. So Ali and his store were on the gang's 'protected' list along with the old lady who lived on her own and liked to feed them scraps and the young lady with three small children whose husband died in the war in Afghanistan.

So that was it. There was Don Schnauzer, The Professor, little Chalkie, Jimmy, Max, Rhavi and Ringo. Oh yes, and there was Paddy. Late as usual, Paddy was missing because he was always missing. Always late, anyway. He was an Irish setter and a great runner, very fast. He would come racing up like an intercity express train, slide to a halt on his hind legs, hunch his shoulders contritely and say, 'Sorry'. But he was always there when he was *really* needed.

Paddy was born in Belfast. He lived there until his owner's work brought him and the rest of the family to the North East. But they had all retained their Irish accents, even the cat. Paddy didn't bother much with her. He thought she was the moodiest moggy he had ever met. And she was mean, too. Paddy liked skimmed milk and their owner would often put out two bowls, one for him and one for her. But if she got there first she would scoff the lot, though she would always deny it.

Ringo, who took his job of summoning members very seriously, told him, 'You should have been here at nine thirty'.

'Why?' Paddy asked innocently. 'What happened?'

'Nothing happened. We were waiting for you.'

'Sure an' I'm here now, so I am.'

The Professor looked around, checking everyone was present. This was a 'special' meeting, not like the usual Friday morning meetings, and they were curious to know what it was all about.

'Brothers,' The Professor began solemnly, 'the King Charles dog who lives in one of the big houses on Park Place has requested an audience with our Dogfather. Don Schnauzer has agreed to meet with her here at ten o'clock. He would like you all to be present to hear what she has to say and he would like you all to behave in a civil and courteous manner.'

Paddy's tail wagged. 'Stuck up girl, so she is.'

'A courteous and civil manner, Paddy,' The Professor cautioned. 'If she does not behave with the proper respect I am sure Don Schnauzer will send her away with a flea in her ear.'

‘I had a flea in my ear once,’ Ringo said. ‘Dead itchy it was.’

‘I had worms,’ someone else said.

‘Order!’ The Professor called and Don Schnauzer nodded at Jimmy. It was almost ten o’clock.

Jimmy raced off to the edge of the wood. He hoped the [illegible] would not be late but he guessed she would be. [illegible] are always late, he told himself. But he was wrong. She was already there beneath the pinky white blossom of a flowering cherry.

‘What’s this?’ he demanded. ‘You didn’t say *she* was coming.’

Ria had brought along her friend Lulu, a French poodle.

‘You don’t think I’m going into those woods with you on my own, do you?’

Lulu was already making eyes at Jimmy. ‘I would,’ she said.

‘Well,’ Jimmy said, embarrassed, ‘I don’t know about this.’

‘She’s coming with us,’ Ria said firmly, ‘and that’s that. Now can we go, please?’

Without another word Jimmy turned on his back paws and they followed him into the wood, through the dappled sunlight and along an unworn path where few humans trod.

‘I’m Lulu, by the way,’ Lulu said, glancing pointedly at Ria.

‘I’m sorry,’ Ria said. ‘This is my friend Lulu.’

‘I guessed that,’ Jimmy said and he looked curiously at Lulu as they walked along. ‘You’re walking normally.’

‘Am I?’ she asked, surprised. ‘And how should I be walking?’

‘Well, when you are out with your owner you walk as though you are walking on hot ashes, stepping out with your head in the air as if you are the Queen or something.’

‘I’m a French poodle,’ she reminded him. ‘That’s what we French poodles do. My mistress expects me to walk like that. I only do it when I'm out with her.' She shrugged. 'And if it keeps her happy...'

'And why do you have your hair cut like that?'

'It's called a lion cut.'

'It looks daft,' Jimmy said.

'I know,' she said with a laugh. 'But it's not my idea. That's what they do to poodles.'

Jimmy laughed with her. She was all right, he decided, not a bit like he expected. Ria was frowning. Her friend and this Jimmy were getting along far too well and she was beginning to wish she hadn't brought her.

'Look,' Jimmy said, slowing them down. 'When you meet the Dogfather, don't forget to bow.'

'Bow?' Ria said derisively. 'I'm not bowing to anybody.'

'Well,' Jimmy told her, 'I expect you want something from us, some kind of help, but if you don't show the proper respect to our leader there'll be nothing doing.'

'Bow-wow!' Lulu said with a laugh.

'I mean it,' Jimmy said.

'Course she'll bow,' Lulu said. 'We'll both take a bow.'

Jimmy was getting worried. He felt responsible now. After all, he was the one who arranged this meeting and the poodle was treating the whole thing as one big joke and the King Charles [illegible] was behaving all snooty again.

'How far is this place?' Ria asked irritably.

'Just here,' Jimmy said and he led them through a cluster of bushes into a small clearing.

All heads turned their way.

'Dogfather,' Jimmy said with a formal bow, 'this is Ria and this is Ria's friend Lulu.'

All heads looked from Ria to Lulu and back to Ria.

Don Schnauzer bowed graciously. 'Ladies,' he said.

Lulu curtsied with a smile and reluctantly Ria bowed.

Don Schnauzer came straight to the point. 'I understand you wish to ask a favour.'

He had expected just the one dog, not two, and he was not happy with too many strangers knowing the exact location of the gang's headquarters.

CHAPTER TWO

Ria faced the assembled gang, Lulu by her side. She glanced at her friend Lulu for support, but Lulu was busy making eyes at Jimmy. She looked around the copse, her nose in the air.

They were a motley crew, she decided superciliously. Rather stupid looking, too. This was probably a waste of time. What could this lot do that could possibly make a difference?

'I don't know if this is a good idea,' she said at last. 'Perhaps there's nothing you can do after all.'

Noting the hint of contempt in her voice, Don Schnauzer looked at her from beneath the hair that partially covered his eyes.

'Very well,' he said quietly. 'If you do not wish to tell us what the problem is we cannot help you solve it.'

There was a moment's pause as they waited, ears cocked for her response. Ria was embarrassed now. The Don's simple yet vaguely patronising statement of fact had made her feel that *she* was the stupid one.

'The thing is,' she began and she faltered.

'Go on,' The Don said softly, after a moment.

'Oot with it, lass,' said Chalkie. 'We're all friends here.'

There were nods and murmurs of approval.

'Well, I'm worried,' she said. 'I'm worried about two dogs that have come to my attention. I'm worried they are being ill treated.'

'By their owner?'

Ria nodded. 'A man called Charlie Spence.'

The Professor whispered in Don Schnauzer's ear and The Don looked at Ria. 'We do know of this man,' he told her. 'He breeds dogs at his smallholding down Edgecroft Way.'

'What he does,' Ria said, 'is illegal. It's not allowed.'

'Breeding dogs is not illegal,' The Don said.

'But what he does is,' she insisted. 'He trains them to fight then when they are old enough he sends them off to take part in dogfights in Europe.'

'Where's Europe?' Paddy asked.

'It's up the M1,' Ringo said.

Most of the gang members had heard of this Charlie Spence and most knew him by sight. He was a short bald man with what looked like a permanent scowl. He wore a gold chain around his neck with dogs' teeth dangling from it. He also wore earrings and cheap bracelets and bangles at his wrists, his arms covered with lurid tattoos.

'What are these dogs?' Rhavi asked. 'Pit bulls?'

'Pit bulls are vicious thugs,' Ringo said. 'I got chased by one once.'

'That's rubbish,' Lulu said vehemently. 'Pit bulls aren't all vicious. I used to know one.' She looked all dreamy. 'He was lovely. Got me in trouble. He was the father of my first litter. My owner was furious. But it was no good being mad at me. It wasn't my fault.'

'I bet,' Paddy said.

'It wasn't,' she insisted. 'They shouldn't have allowed me to get out.' She sighed. 'Ah, but he was lovely.'

'No dogs are born vicious,' Max the German shepherd said soberly. 'It's the way they are brought up.'

'Well said, Max,' Chalkie told him.

'Order, order,' The Professor called.

'Brothers.' Don Schnauzer addressed the members of the gang. 'Please allow the lady to tell us what evidence she has that these dogs really are being ill treated and if her claim seems genuine we will, of course, discuss in what way we can help.'

Everyone was quiet now, waiting for Ria to back up her claim.

'Last Sunday afternoon,' Ria began, 'my owner took me for a walk down Edgecroft Way. It was extremely quiet. There was no one about. But as we passed this big old shed on Spence's land we heard Spence shouting and swearing and lashing out with a strap or something. Then there were these terrified squeals. Just awful, it was. And after a while it went quiet and all we could hear was this pathetic little whimpering sound.'

The gang sat in silence, their mouths open, then Chalkie asked, 'Did ye no investigate?'

'Well,' Ria said, 'my owner was very concerned. His name is Robert and he is a true gentleman. He wanted to know what was going on and so did I. But we didn't get very far. There is a big strong gate and if you don't know the code you have to ring a bell for attention. Robert wanted to speak to Spence, but when he rang the bell these two large Rottweilers came bounding up. They looked so wild I thought they were going to jump right over the gate and tear us apart.'

'Drugs,' Ringo said. 'They're probably on drugs.'

'Nah,' Paddy said. 'He's probably got them fighting mad, all wound up.'

'But, give him his due,' Ria went on, 'my man Robert was not frightened. He just kept on ringing the bell until Spence came.'

'He spoke to Spence?' The Professor asked.

'Yes,' she said, 'but Spence was very rude. He just told us go away – but not in those words.'

'He told you to...?' Ringo said.

'All right, Ringo,' The Professor said. 'We can guess what the man said.'

'So we went home and Robert told his wife, Elizabeth. He was going to look into this, he said. He was not going to let the matter rest. But Elizabeth said we should keep out of it. It was nothing to do with us, none of our business. Anyway, on his way home from the office next day, Robert went to the police station and spoke to the sergeant. He was told that he would have to make an official complaint – so he did.'

'And what happened?' The Professor asked.

'Nothing, as far as I know,' she said. 'The sergeant said they would look into it but I don't know that they have. Nothing seems to be happening.'

'We heard there were some police dogs at the station last Friday,' Lulu said, 'so we went to see them and we told them what was going on. They promised they would see what they could do, but their officers were very busy.'

'They were not much use,' Ria said scornfully and she looked at Lulu accusingly. 'I expect they had forgotten what we went for after you had finished rolling around with them.'

Lulu smiled sweetly.

'Well now,' Don Schnauzer said, 'it doesn't look as if we have very much to go on here. Your owner thinks this Spence fellow is training young pit bulls to be fighting dogs, but you don't have any proof that this is so.'

'It's true,' Ria protested. 'Lots of people in the village know about it, but Spence is a violent man. People are scared of him.'

'I'm not,' Paddy said, sticking his chest out and posing for Lulu's benefit. 'I'm not afraid of any man.'

'All right, Paddy,' The Professor said, 'we'll bear that in mind.'

'He has to be stopped,' Ria said. 'If you had heard those little dogs whimpering...' Her voice trailed.

Don Schnauzer nodded. 'Thank you, my dear,' he said. 'We will discuss this matter and look at all the options. And then, if possible, we will devise a plan of action.'

The Professor stood up to indicate the meeting was over.

'One of you must escort these ladies out of the wood,' The Don ordered and Jimmy stood up, but The Don said quickly, 'Not you, Jimmy. I want you here.'

'I'll do it, boss,' Paddy volunteered.

The Don nodded. 'And Paddy,' he said. 'Come straight back.'

'Yes, boss,' Paddy said reluctantly, and as he led Ria and Lulu from the copse, Ria turned and gave Jimmy her best smile.

'Ooh!' several voices murmured and Jimmy was embarrassed.

'Gather round,' The Don said when they had gone. 'So what do we actually know about this Charlie Spence?'

'There *is* a lot of talk in the village,' Rhavi said. 'I've heard people going on about him in the store, but nobody seems to know for sure what he's up to. I think it's true. He *is* a nasty character and everybody's scared of him.'

'Well, we're not,' Ringo said. 'No way.'

'Order!' The Professor called and everyone looked at The Don.

The Don turned to The Professor and whispered something in his ear. The Professor nodded and whispered something back and for several seconds they consulted in whispers. Then The Don's hair-fringed eyes looked out at the assembled gang.

Perhaps it was to keep the hair from his mouth, but The Don always spoke as if he was wearing a gumshield. 'We understand this man's premises are guarded and patrolled day and night,' he began, 'by two large Rottweilers. If we are to have any hope of rescuing these unfortunate dogs we need to get to know these guards, find out what their attitude is towards Spence and find out if they approve or disapprove of what he's doing. Or, for that matter, if they actually *know* what he's doing.'

'They probably don't,' Ringo said. 'Rottweilers are pretty thick.'

'Oh, I don't know about that,' Rhavi said. 'I remember when...'

'Order!' The Professor called.

'It may be,' The Don went on, 'that the Rottweilers are open to persuasion. We might be able to recruit them as allies, get them on our side.' He looked around as if deciding who to give the job to, but in fact he had already made up his mind. He looked at The Professor and said quietly, 'We'll give this job to Jimmy.'

Jimmy was thrilled to be given such an important assignment. He hadn't been a member of the gang all that long and being trusted with a job like this made him feel that now he really was part of the team.

He remembered when he first joined and he was feeling a bit unsure of himself. Ringo the beagle had asked him, not in a nasty way or anything, what his pedigree was. This was quite a posh area where they all lived. Park Place was at the more expensive end of the village and all the dogs and all the ladies, too, had quite impressive pedigrees. He had hesitated, a little embarrassed, when Ringo asked but Paddy had come to the rescue.

'Sure an' he's a mixed breed,' Paddy told him. 'He has the brains of two breeds when you don't even have the brains you were born wit'.'

The Professor had told Jimmy he should try to talk to the two Rottweilers separately. 'Get them apart if you can,' he said in his careful ponderous voice. 'No two dogs are the same, not even Rottweilers. You must find out which is the stronger of the two, which one is the leader. Then, if you can, speak to him alone.'

Jimmy had left the copse and was walking back across the field to the main road when he met Paddy who was only just returning from escorting the bitches.

'The meeting's over,' Jimmy said, with a smile.

'Well, that's all right, then,' Paddy said and he turned around and fell in beside him.

'I'm glad I've seen you, Jimmy,' he said, after a moment. 'There's something I want to ask you.'

Jimmy looked at him quizzically.

'About that dog,' Paddy went on. 'You know – Lulu.'

'What about her?' Jimmy asked.

'Do you mind if I walk out with her?'

'Mind?' Jimmy said. 'Why would I mind?'

'Well, I thought she might be your girl.'

Jimmy laughed. 'No, of course she isn't. She's not my type.'

'Are you sure?'

'Sure I'm sure,' Jimmy said. 'She's a nice girl. I like her, but she's not for me. She's all yours.'

Paddy nodded, obviously pleased. 'Right,' he said, then he gave Jimmy a knowing look. 'I get it. It's the other one, isn't it? The stuck... I mean, the spaniel – Ria.'

Jimmy denied it. 'She isn't mine either. I don't have a girl.'

'I bet,' Paddy said, unconvinced.

They parted with a raised paw at the edge of the village. But Jimmy didn't go home. He carried on down the lane towards Edgecroft and Charlie Spence's smallholding. He had a job to do now and he wanted to make a start right away.

There was a bank of daffodils along one side of the lane and there were crocuses and primroses in the gardens of the houses. Here and there, too, were freshly planted shrubs with the name tags still attached. All this added to the feeling of a freshness, a *new*ness in the air and Jimmy felt it keenly.

Perhaps Paddy's gentle teasing had awakened his heart to the possibilities ahead for he felt a sudden urge to run and jump and fall over and roll in the growing grass.

He was young and alive. He had a good home, loyal friends and the respect of people he admired. Now he had a cause, something to fight for, and he felt just then that anything he wanted was within his grasp. It was a feeling of overwhelming joy and anticipation. And little did he realise he might never feel this way again.

There were fewer homes as he drew near to Charlie Spence's place, then there was only one, a bungalow, on the enclosed land where Spence lived. There seemed to be no one about. It was very quiet, so quiet that even the soft padding of his paws on the dirt road had alerted one of the guard dogs.

Jimmy could see him out of the corner of his eye. He was a big Rottweiler and through the strong wire netting that enclosed the smallholding the Rottweiler was watching his every move. Jimmy didn't look at the Rottweiler. He simply sat down on the gently rising grassy bank opposite.

'Hey!' the Rottweiler cried, after a moment.

Jimmy looked around, unconcerned, then he looked directly across at the Rottweiler. With his nose slightly raised and his voice mildly challenging, he said, 'Are you talking to me?'

The Rottweiler's eyes narrowed. Other dogs were supposed to be scared of him, but this one wasn't and he didn't like it. This one, he decided, was going to have to be put in his place.

'What do you want?' he barked.

'What's it to you?' Jimmy asked.

'I ask the questions around here,' the Rottweiler said, a little less sure of himself.

'Ask away,' Jimmy said.

'What's your name?'

'Jimmy,' Jimmy told him. 'What's yours?'

'Er...' The Rottweiler looked even less sure of himself.

'Come on,' Jimmy said. 'I told you mine.'

'It's Rocky,' the Rottweiler said.

The other guard dog had appeared now. He had heard their voices. He was standing, erect and alert, by the bungalow and he was looking up towards the gate.

'Rocky?' Jimmy said with a laugh. 'And I suppose he's Rambo.'

The Rottweiler called Rocky bristled. 'You trying to take the...'

'No, no,' Jimmy said, still smiling. 'It's just that it's the sort of name someone like Charlie Spence *would* give him.'

'Well, it is. Yeah. He's Rambo. And he's a killer.'

'Rambo's a killer?' Jimmy questioned. 'And why is that?'

'You got to be tough to do our job.'

'Is that right?' Jimmy said. 'And are you a killer?'

'Well...' Rocky hesitated.

'Of course you're not. And neither is Rambo. I bet you are quite nice fellows really. You think Rottweilers are supposed to be scary so you act tough.'

'That's our job. We have to be scary to protect the place and stop anyone trying to break in.'

'And finding out what Charlie Spence is up to?'

‘What do you mean by that?’

Jimmy decided they had been getting along fine up to now. He didn’t want to say too much and spoil things. ‘It’s nothing to do with me,’ he said, ‘but you know what they are like in the village. You hear things.’

‘Like what?’

‘Well,’ Jimmy said, ‘they reckon what Charlie does is not legal.’

‘What are you talking about?’

‘It may not be true, of course, but they say he breeds pit bulls and turns them into fighting dogs. You know, for dogfights.’

‘That’s what pit bulls do.’

‘No, it isn’t,’ Jimmy said testily. ’Pit bulls are not fighters. They are only made that way by people like your boss. They are badly beaten and starved until they’re ravenous. Then they are made to fight each other for food. And when they’re ready, when they are *really* wild, they are taken to dogfights. They are forced to fight other dogs while morons like Charlie Spence and his stupid mates put bets on which one will survive. Sometimes, quite often in fact, it’s a fight to the death.’

Rocky knew in a vague way that this was true, but he had never really thought about it. Now that he did think about it, he knew it was wrong and somehow shameful. He didn’t know what to say.

Jimmy decided he himself had said too much. ‘Listen, Rocky,’ he said quietly, ‘none of this has anything to do with me.’

‘No,’ Rocky said, ‘it hasn’t.’

‘Anyway,’ Jimmy told him, ‘I’d like us to be friends. It was good talking to you and I like it down here. It’s nice and quiet. Maybe I can come by again, say hello. That is, if you don’t mind.’

Rocky looked at him for a moment then seemed to make up his mind. 'Yeah, why not?' Then he added, 'I don't know if it would be all right with Mr Spence though, he's not keen on visitors. Best not to let him see you.'

Jimmy laughed. 'You think he might grab me and turn me into a raving mad dogfighter?'

'Not you. You're not the type.'

'I told you,' Jimmy said, standing up to go. 'No dog is the type. It's what some evil humans turn them into. See you, Rocky.'

He went on his way, pleased with this first contact. But he wasn't thinking about Rottweilers. He couldn't stop thinking about Ria.

CHAPTER THREE

Jimmy was to report his progress, if any, at the copse. The Don and The Professor, but none of the others, were there and, clearly impressed that he had made contact so soon, they listened intently as he told them of his encounter with Rocky the Rottweiler.

'You have done well, Jimmy,' The Don said, nodding sagely. 'I am sure you can build on this relationship. But we must proceed with caution. I think the next step may be to involve the other guard dog, find out if he is likely to be a friend or a foe.'

The Professor coughed to indicate he had something to say. 'Dogfather,' he said respectfully, 'our spies tell us that this Spence person comes up to the village every Wednesday afternoon. He comes on other days, of course, but he never misses Wednesday afternoons. He buys provisions at the village store, loads up his van, then he goes in the Black Bull and stays there until about seven in the evening, sometimes later. He's been barred from the pub twice now and the landlord says this is absolutely his last chance to behave himself or he'll be banned for life.'

Besides the Black Bull there were two other public houses in Warkwood and Charlie Spence had been barred from both of them. The only other bars were in the hotels, The Warkwood House and The Sun, and Spence had been barred from both since he came to the village six years ago.

'How does a man get himself barred from a public house?' Jimmy asked.

'In Spence's case,' The Professor said, 'he's rude and insulting. He upsets the ladies and his language is atrocious.'

'Then we must act before he does get himself barred,' The Don told them. 'The day after tomorrow is Wednesday, Jimmy. Time to make your second call.'

Jimmy bowed, accepting The Don's instructions graciously. He was quite keen to go back. He felt he had established a rapport with Rocky, something he could build on. He felt he could talk to him, maybe talk him round. But the other guard dog could be a problem. How to deal with Rambo? That was the question. On the way home he ran into Rhavi.

'Hey, Jimmy. How are you doing?'

'I'm fine, Rhavi. You okay?'

Rhavi was rolling over, shaking with laughter. 'Guess what?' he said at last. 'I've just seen that crazy setter – Paddy. He's strutting around the village with that poncy poodle in tow.'

'I would have thought Lulu would have *Paddy* in tow.'

'You're right. She's the boss. No doubt about that. And I'll tell you what. She's a real handful that Lulu. She'll lead him a rare old dance and then she'll dump him. Just like that.'

'Maybe we should warn him,' Jimmy said.

'Too late,' Rhavi said. 'He's crazy about her.'

It was a Monday afternoon and it was quiet in the village. The children were in school and the little park, usually so alive with shouts and laughter, was empty. Although, it was not quite empty. As Jimmy went by he spotted Paddy and Lulu.

Lulu was walking around as she did when she was out with her owner. She was doing that silly walk that poodles do, with her nose in the air and a look of disdain for anyone and everyone. Paddy was dancing along beside and around her, like a moth to a flame. Then he saw Jimmy and he started to bark.

'Hey, Jimmy!' he cried. 'Over here.'

Jimmy ambled casually between the big iron gates as they came towards him. Lulu immediately began to preen herself and pose and flutter her eyelashes, her head on one side with a coy smile.

‘Well hello, Jimmy,’ she said seductively.

Paddy stepped between them. ‘We’ve got a message for you,’ he said. ‘That Ria wants to see you.’

‘She knows where I live,’ Jimmy said.

‘She’s not going to come looking for you,’ Lulu told him. ‘She’s much too proud for that.’

‘It’s all right, so it is,’ Paddy said. ‘She cannot get out just now. There’s something going on at their house. Today and tomorrow she’s wanted there. Relatives visiting or something like that. But Wednesday is okay. She said she’ll see you Wednesday if you go along to her place at two o’clock.’

‘Can’t do that,’ Jimmy said. ‘I’m busy on Wednesday.’

‘Ooh!’ Lulu made a face as if to say ‘Get him!’

‘She won’t be very pleased, Jim,’ Paddy said.

‘I have some important business to attend to,’ he said.

‘More important than Ria?’

Jimmy threw Paddy a look. ‘It’s *mob* business.’

Paddy nodded, understanding, as Jimmy turned to leave.

Jimmy looked back and smiled. ‘You better watch out for this smooth-talker, Lulu,’ he warned. ‘He’s full of the old blarney.’

‘I can handle him, no problem,’ Lulu said confidently and she turned to Paddy and said, ‘Sit!’

Paddy grinned and obediently sat down.

Jimmy couldn’t wait for Wednesday afternoon. He spent most of Monday evening and all day Tuesday thinking up imaginary conversations between himself and the Rottweilers. Yet when the time came and he set off down the lane to Spence’s smallholding, he had no idea what he was going to say.

It had rained quite heavily during the night and the lane was dotted with puddles. Now, as he walked along, deep in thought, he was suddenly startled by a van that came hurtling full speed towards him. He jumped out of harm's way but the van driver deliberately went through a deep puddle with the clear intention of soaking him to the skin.

The driver was laughing as if this was a great joke and Jimmy was not surprised to see it was Charlie Spence. It was just the sort of thing a man like Spence would do. 'Birdbrain,' Jimmy murmured. But then he thought no, that's not fair to birds.

The Professor had said that humans are 'creatures of habit' and it was true. That was Spence going off on his weekly ritual. Every Wednesday. Village store then the Black Bull. Jimmy had been thinking about things more deeply recently and it was probably The Professor's influence. What The Professor said always made sense and he made you think about things and the way things are.

The other day, for instance, Jimmy had caught sight of himself in a shop window and this had reminded him that he was not like the other dogs around Park Place. They were all *pedigree* dogs. They shared their looks with the rest of the breed they belonged to. This had bothered him a bit at first, but when he mentioned it to The Professor, The Professor had told him he should be grateful and proud to be himself, not a carbon copy of a gang of look-alikes.

Jimmy's father, from what he had heard, was a Border collie. He was a fine dog and he had a good job as a shepherd. Jimmy's mother, apparently, was a Manchester terrier. Her owners had taken her on a caravan holiday to the Dales and she had been allowed to play freely in the Yorkshire countryside.

Jimmy smiled to himself as he walked along. My dad must have been quite a dog, he thought. Even though he was working full-time, shepherding two flocks of sheep, he still found time to get to know my mother and so she came home with rather more than a few holiday memories.

He wished he had known his father. He had so many of his father's characteristics. He was mainly black and white where a Manchester terrier, like his mother, is black and tan. He also had a white chest and the lower halves of his legs were white. That crazy poodle, Lulu, had laughed at his legs and asked him why he wore white socks. He had laughed back and said, 'I have no choice but you don't *have* to wear those silly pompoms.'

It seemed to Jimmy that, in many ways, he had been lucky. He had a smooth black and white coat and a flowing black and white tail. He had the best of both his parents, yet he knew he was not prized by humans. Humans preferred to pay lots of money for pedigree dogs that looked more or less the same as the rest of their breed. As The Professor said, 'They are conformists all of them and, like our woolly friend, the sheep, they will follow the flock no matter what.' None of this mattered, Jimmy told himself. After all, he had never had any problem attracting the [illegible] girls

He was quite a big dog, too, more like his Border collie dad than his Manchester terrier mother. In fact, he was not all that much smaller than Rocky the Rottweiler.

It was a pleasant day. The night's rain had gone and the early afternoon sun was shining in the puddles. Now, as he drew near the wire netting in search of Rocky, he heard a low warning growl, a growl that was clearly intended to be scary. Undeterred he went straight to the fence and confronted the angry Rottweiler.

'What's the problem, Rambo?' he asked, his head on one side to reflect his concern. 'You got toothache or something?'

The Rottweiler stood back and looked at him in surprise. 'How do you know my name?'

'Well,' Jimmy said, 'I guess a big strong, fine-looking dog like you *would* be called Rambo.'

Rambo stood tall, preening himself. 'Yeah, that's right,' he said.

Good, thought Jimmy. He's as dumb as he looks.

It was just then that Rocky appeared, clearly pleased to see him.

'Hey, Rocky!' Jimmy called out and Rocky returned his greeting.

'You two know each other?' Rambo asked, with a frown.

'Yeah,' Rocky said. 'Jimmy's a friend of mine.'

'Not a bad day today,' Jimmy said. 'Can't be much fun being cooped up behind that wire.'

'Ah, but we're not,' Rocky told him. 'It's Wednesday today. The boss is always away for a few hours on Wednesday so we go for a little walk around the village, scare a few people. Don't we, Rambo?'

Rambo was nodding his head and grinning idiotically.

'And why would you want to do that?' Jimmy asked, as if he was genuinely puzzled.

'It's good fun,' Rocky said defensively. 'Folk see two Rottweilers strolling around and they're scared. They call their children in and all the other dogs and cats go running home. It's hilarious!'

'Doesn't sound much fun,' Jimmy said, 'everybody hating you. And you don't get to know any of the children. Little kids are good fun, Rocky. And they love us dogs. Most of us, anyway.'

Rocky was a slow thinker and this obviously hadn't occurred to him. He was quiet now, thinking it over.

'I bet you're having me on,' Jimmy said, with a laugh. 'There's no way you can get out of there. It's like a prison camp.'

'Ah, but there is,' Rocky said, brightening. 'Here! I'll show you.'

Rocky went along the wire netting with Jimmy following on the other side. Then, when he was out of view of Spence's bungalow and close to where a line of conifers began to screen the fence, he came to a halt. On the ground close to the wire netting was a piece of plywood. Rocky drew this aside to reveal a hole wide enough for him or Rambo to crawl through. On the other side of the wire netting the hole was hidden by a large square of turf and several dead branches.

Rocky wriggled through the hole expertly, as though he had done this many times, and he pushed the turf aside to emerge triumphant. 'You coming, Rambo?' he asked, over his shoulder.

'Yeah,' Rambo said and he, too, wriggled through.

The three dogs stood facing each other in an awkward triangle.

'What are we gonna do now?' Rambo asked.

'We could go for a walk,' Jimmy suggested, 'towards the village.'

'Yeah,' Rocky said. 'Scare some kids.'

'Whoa! No way!' Jimmy said. 'You're not going to scare *any* kids. Not if you're with me, you're not. You're not going to scare anybody.'

'But that's what we do,' Rocky protested. 'We scare people.'

'Yeah,' Rambo said emphatically. 'That's what we do.'

'And that's why you have no friends, why nobody likes you,' Jimmy told them. 'They're all scared of you. They won't let their children anywhere near you.'

'So?' Rocky queried.

'Well, it's very sad,' Jimmy said. 'I mean, doesn't it get boring? The same old thing week after week. Scaring people off. Folk running away. Believe me, it's much more fun and much nicer being popular.'

'Yeah?' Rambo's face was contorted as he struggled to take this in.

Jimmy smiled. 'Let's go towards the village and if we come across anyone, grown-ups or children, I'll show you how to make friends.'

'I don't know if we're *supposed* to make friends,' Rocky said doubtfully. 'We're Rottweilers. People are *supposed* to be scared of us.'

'Why?' Jimmy demanded. 'Because you would be no good as guard dogs? Is that what you think? Well, you're wrong. I mean, if people liked you and were not scared of you it wouldn't matter. Most people don't do anything wrong anyway. But if one of them did, like, say, a burglar tried to break into old Spence's place...'

'Better not!' Rambo said fiercely.

'Exactly,' Jimmy said. 'You would only have to growl and bare your teeth and he'd be off like a shot. What I'm saying is, you only have to be scary when it's really necessary, when it's part of your job.'

'Oh, I dunno,' Rocky said, still unconvinced. 'Folk are supposed to be scared of Rottweilers and that's what we are.'

Rambo nodded in agreement.

'That's rubbish,' Jimmy argued. 'It's just idiots like Spence who tell you you're supposed to frighten people.'

Rocky was listening intently and Rambo was looking at Rocky, waiting for a lead. Jimmy knew this was it. If they turned on him now he was in trouble.

'Listen,' he said softly. 'Let's just walk down the lane and, if we meet anyone, you watch what I do.'

Rocky looked at him for a long moment then nodded, making his mind up. Rambo just looked puzzled.

Three abreast they set off walking slowly down the lane and they didn't have long to wait for Jimmy to go into action. A young man and a little boy were coming up the lane towards them.

'Watch me,' Jimmy said quietly.

The little boy was about three years old, new to the joy of running ahead without restraints. The young man was the boy's father and he spotted the three quite large dogs immediately.

'Bobbie!' he called nervously, but the boy went on running. The boy's father quickened his pace, his call more urgent. 'Bobbie!'

Rocky and Rambo slowed down now as Jimmy went forward to meet the little boy. The boy put out a hand and immediately Jimmy lowered his head and allowed the boy to stroke him.

The boy's father had realised that both the bigger dogs were Rottweilers. His face was pale and apprehensive, but the little boy, totally unaware of any tension, laughed happily. Jimmy gently nuzzled his nose into the boy's midriff and the boy's hands went around his silky neck.

Jimmy lay down now and rolled over and the boy fell on top of him. The boy's father waited, not sure what to do, his eyes darting from the Rottweilers to Jimmy and his little boy who was sitting astride Jimmy's upturned body. Slowly, gently, Jimmy eased himself upright as the little boy put both arms around his neck and gave him a big hug.

'Come along, Bobbie,' the boy's father said. 'Nice doggie, but we have to go now.'

Jimmy looked back at Rocky and indicated that he should join in. Rocky came forward slowly then gently nuzzled his head into the little boy's chest. The little boy laughed and, squealing with delight, he put both his arms around Rocky's neck.

'He loves you, Rocky,' Jimmy whispered softly.

Rocky's eyes were shining and, looking on, Rambo wanted to get in on the action. He lay down and rolled over on the grassy bank. Rocky laughed. 'Come on, you dope,' he said. 'Not over there. Come here where he can give you a hug.'

Bashfully Rambo sidled up to the boy, his head down, and was rewarded with a huge hug. Both Rottweilers were on their backs now, feet in the air, and the boy was laughing and falling about between them. Jimmy couldn't believe it. These two were not big vicious thugs at all. They were a couple of softies.

The boy's father, still a little apprehensive, tried again. 'Come along now, Bobbie. We have to go.' Then, tentatively, he put his hand out and patted Rambo. Revelling in the attention, Rambo lowered his head affectionately.

To the dogs, unaware that they could understand every word, the young man said, 'We'll come and see you fine fellows again, won't we, Bobbie?'

He took the boy by the hand and gently but firmly drew him away. 'What lovely, dogs,' he said. 'What lovely well-behaved dogs. They're a credit to their owner, aren't they, son?'

'Don't know about that,' Rocky murmured under his breath.

Jimmy and the others drew back but the boy wanted to hug each one of them once more and he did and they loved it.

The boy's father laughed. 'Now come on. Wave bye-bye.'

The little boy held out an arm, his chubby fingers opening and closing. 'Bye-bye,' he cried and he kept looking back, his arm still outstretched. 'Bye-bye.'

All three bowed their heads and, backing off, they turned and went on their way.

'Poor man was scared stiff,' Jimmy said.

'No need to be scared of us,' Rocky said.

'Nah,' Rambo said. 'That's right.'

'He's a nice little kid that Bobbie,' Rocky said, clearly thrilled by the encounter. 'I never had a big hug before.'

'Neither have I,' Rambo said.

'Never?' Jimmy said, surprised. 'That's sad.'

'All we ever get from Spence is a kick if we get in his way or if we're not where he thinks we should be.' Rocky was frowning at the injustice. 'I reckon a big hug from a little kid like Bobbie is much better than scaring him.'

'So do I,' Rambo agreed, equally delighted. 'I reckon he liked me best. You could tell.'

'No way!' Rocky told him. 'He wouldn't let *me* go.'

'All right, all right,' Jimmy said, peacemaking. 'It was pretty obvious he liked both of you. And it hasn't changed you, has it? You can still scare people who need scaring. But you can be nice, too.'

Rocky came to a halt as they neared the first row of village houses. 'We'd better not go any further,' he said. 'We don't want to frighten anyone.'

Jimmy nodded. 'Okay. I'll come and see you soon.'

'Yeah,' Rocky agreed. 'You do that.'

'Wait a minute,' Rambo said. 'What do you do? You roll over with your feet in the air...'

'No, no,' Rocky told him. 'You go up to someone real calm, not a bit threatening, and you put your head down so it's pretty obvious you want them to stroke you and, whatever you do, you don't show your teeth. It's then, when they can see that you're all sort of friendly and everything, you can roll over and put your feet in the air. It helps them to relax and, you never know, you might get a big hug.'

‘That’s it, Rocky,’ Jimmy told him. ‘You’ve got it.’

‘You put your head down and you don’t show your teeth,’ Rambo told himself.

‘See you,’ Jimmy called and he wagged his tail happily as he turned and went on his way.

CHAPTER FOUR

Don Schnauzer was delighted with Jimmy's progress. After only two meetings with the Rottweilers, Jimmy had done far better than could have been expected.

In his muffled voice The Don told Jimmy, 'We must still go carefully. We must gain their confidence and friendship even more. It would be a mistake to take them for granted or to expect their co-operation too soon. Perhaps another couple of Wednesday afternoons.'

'Would it be a good idea to invite them here, to the copse?' The Professor asked tentatively. 'If they were to make friends with all of us...'

'We could invite them to the concert,' Chalkie suggested.

'I don't know about that,' Don Schnauzer said.

'That might put them off us completely,' The Professor said.

From time to time the gang entertained each other, and any of the local dogs who wished to attend, with a concert by a stretch of the river that was hidden from view by a small but densely wooded area of maple and poplar trees.

Ringo wanted to form a dog band but none of the others could sing in tune or even bark on the beat and he was forever holding auditions. There were always plenty of hopefuls from the surrounding villages but he had not yet found any potential pop stars. He would invariably end up on his own on the improvised stage doing his Elvis impressions These were good but they were getting a bit boring, even to him, so he had become a bit more adventurous recently. He was working on a new routine where he tried to dance and move like Michael Jackson.

Rhavi did tricks like a magician. He was pretty good and he could do some unbelievable things with a bone. After the last concert though he was told off by The Don for causing trouble in the village. As part of his act he had shown the audience how to unclip a lead and some of them had gone wild, freeing themselves and running into the road and causing accidents.

Paddy, of course, had to get in on the act with his stand-up comedy routine and his Irish songs. It was mostly jokes about daft Irish dogs and the songs he got from his favourite band, The Drop-Kick Murphys.

'When is the next concert?' The Don asked.

'Week on Wednesday,' Chalkie, who was the organiser and producer of the concerts, told him.

But Jimmy was not interested in the concerts. He could think of little else now but rescuing those poor pit bulls. Every week that went by, he realised, they would be getting bigger, stronger, meaner, wilder and more ready to fight. The longer they left it the more difficult it would be to rescue them and get them into a family that would love them and take care of them and treat them with respect.

He was sitting at home now, watching *Coronation Street* with his owners, Arthur and Doreen. They were a quiet couple with no children, and they never seemed to have much to do in the evenings. They both went out to work every day but they didn't say much about their jobs and Jimmy had no idea what kind of work they did. But Jimmy had no complaints.

Though they were not exactly affectionate, they took good care of him, always made sure there was something in his bowl and his water basin. But they rarely took him for a walk or anything. They may have been too tired when they got home from work during the week, and at weekends there was always some excuse.

They overslept or it was raining, always something. Saturday Arthur went to the football and Doreen went to the shops. And another thing – they both drank too much, Arthur with his cans of beer, Doreen with her bottles of wine. But they were all right. He had plenty of free time and he could always get out during the day. A small window in the outhouse was left off the latch and they knew he could get in or out that way.

Jimmy liked *Coronation Street*. He liked most of the soaps, but he liked *Corrie* best because there was a big dog in it called Schmeicel. Tonight *Coronation Street* was mostly about a rather pretty girl called Maria and this reminded him of Ria, the King Charles spaniel.

He hadn't seen much of her recently. In fact, he hadn't seen her at all since the day she came to the meeting in the copse. He decided, out of politeness if nothing else, he ought to tell her he was working on the Pit Bull case and he was making progress. He wouldn't tell her too much about it, of course. He would just say that he was working on it.

'Hey, Paddy,' he cried when next they met. 'Still seeing Lulu?'

'Oh sure,' Paddy said with a big grin. 'She's a great girl, so she is. Always up to something.'

'Well, will you ask her to bring Ria along next time you see her? We can go for a walk, the four of us.'

'Where to?'

'I don't know, do I?' Jimmy said. 'Anywhere. Down by the river somewhere. But not Wednesday. I can't do Wednesdays.'

There were several meadows around the village where they could take a walk: Parish Field, Daisy Bank, Spring Meadow. Parish Field was probably the best. It was just by the parish church, a stretch of green that ran alongside the river. It was where the children lined up for the Easter Walks. It was where the scouts and guides and brownies and cubs assembled on St George's Day. It was where the May Day Parade began when a girl from the village was crowned May Queen. And it was where the British Legion paid their respects on Armistice Day.

On Sundays in summer, families, usually with small children, would picnic there and small boys and girls, and some not so small, would fish with rods and nets along the river bank.

'I think Parish is best,' Paddy said.

'Spring is quieter.'

'Yeah, but Parish is nearer home for Lulu and Ria, so it is. They may not be allowed out for long.'

'Right,' Jimmy said. 'Parish it is.'

Paddy lost no time and the very next day the four of them were out walking by the river on Parish Field. Paddy and Lulu walked ahead, very close, as if they had been drawn together by a magnet. Jimmy and Ria walked apart. Ria aloof and pointedly cool.

'I'm sorry I haven't been in touch,' he said. 'I've been so busy.'

'Oh yes?' Ria said, as if to say: What do I care?

'I've been working, as a matter of fact, on the case. But I can't tell you much about it at this stage. Progress is slow. It has to be, I'm afraid, if we're going to get anywhere.'

Ria looked at him with interest. 'The case?'

'The pit bulls at Charlie Spence's place. We're working on a way to set them free.'

'Oh,' she said and she softened somewhat. 'I see.'

'It's pretty dangerous work, Ria, but now that I've started I want to see it through. It's something I really want to do.'

He told her how he had met and made friends with the two Rottweilers, how he hoped they would help free the pit bulls.

Ria came closer, their coats almost touching. She looked up at him earnestly. 'I wouldn't want you to get hurt,' she said.

Paddy and Lulu had walked on ahead and Jimmy noticed Ria was walking much slower, not making any effort to catch up.

They were on a long stretch of grass that ran between the river and the road. Along the road there was a bright yellow display of daffodils. Across the road was Park Row and the large, rather posh houses where Ria and Lulu were next door neighbours.

Parish Field was protected land, couldn't be built on, Ria said. It belonged to The National Trust. Jimmy had never heard of The National Trust. They protect the most beautiful parts of Britain, Ria explained. So this must be one of the most beautiful parts of Britain.

'It is today,' Jimmy said.

Ria looked at him sidelong, her eyes softened. 'Why today?'

'Because you're in it,' he said.

She laughed and ran away and he chased her. He could easily have caught her but he didn't want to. He just wanted to run and jump and roll over and enjoy the green of the grass, the yellow of the flowers and the bluey-grey sheen of the gently flowing river.

Ria collapsed and rolled over and Jimmy lay down beside her. She seemed such a lady he didn't dare touch her, but she turned to him and nestled against him and they lay quite still, looking up at the clear blue sky.

There was a squawking sound close by and they rolled over, crouching low like snipers in the grass, to take a look. A stately duck was leading a line of ducklings along the river bank as if they were on a supervised outing and on their best behaviour.

'Do you think they have names?' Ria asked in a whisper.

'I expect so,' Jimmy whispered back. 'We do.'

'Yes, but our names are given to us by our owners. Who would give them their names?'

‘I dunno,’ Jimmy said. ‘Their mother, I expect.’

Ria lay back again in the long grass. ‘Do you go for walks?’

‘Sometimes,’ Jimmy said. ‘I know the village pretty well. Every corner of it, I should think. We all do.’

‘I don’t,’ Ria said wistfully. ‘It’s not fair really. You seem to be able to go out whenever you like. I always have to go for walks with Robert or Elizabeth, sometimes both. It’s mostly Robert actually, and I’m always on a lead.’

‘They must love you,’ he said. ‘Scared of losing you, I expect.’

‘Oh, they do,’ she said. ‘Don’t yours love you?’

‘I think they do,’ Jimmy said. ‘They just don’t show it much.’

‘You should get them to take you for walks. You would enjoy it. Robert has taken me on some great walks. We go up to the ruins sometimes and one day there was a guide telling us about the history of the castle and the Hermitage and what went on there. It was very interesting.’

Ria was lying back now and Jimmy rolled over to look down into her eyes.

‘It’s interesting to think that in the olden days the knights wore those great heavy suits of armour,’ she said. ‘It’s a wonder they could walk with all that weight. Battle helmets and breastplates and things like that.’

‘I bet the dogs didn’t wear armour,’ Jimmy said.

‘Of course they didn’t, you daft thing,’ she said, smiling at the thought. ‘But if you would like to see one. A real suit of armour, I mean. There’s one in the church. If you wander into St Lawrence’s Church in the village when there’s no one to shoo you off, you’ll find there’s one standing in the corner just inside the door. A knight in a real suit of armour.’

'I'll take a look,' Jimmy said, though he was more interested just then in looking into Ria's eyes.

'I think it's funny,' she said, 'that all through the ages people have worn different styles of dress, different fashions, and made themselves look different. Suits and ties and ladies in trousers. Everything changes, all the time. Yet we always look the same. A dog in the days of the Roman Empire, and before that even, looked just the same as we do.'

'The people are the same,' Jimmy said. 'It's just the clothes that change. People seem to spend most of their time looking at clothes. They spend hours in shops deciding what to buy then when they get home they don't like what they've bought.'

'Lulu's mistress is the worst,' Ria said. 'She has dozens of suits and dresses and thousands of shoes and handbags.'

Jimmy laughed. 'I bet Lulu would have, too, if she could.'

'Anyway, she said, 'you should get your man to take you on some walks. Get a leaflet for the Cook and Barker and put it somewhere where he can't miss it.'

'The Cook and Barker?'

'It's a lovely pub in a place called Newton on the Moor. Just off the A1. We always go there Boxing Day for the foxhunt.'

'I thought foxhunting was banned.'

'It is. But the hunt still meets there and it's a wonderful sight. Beautiful horses and huntsmen in their bright red coats and all those handsome dogs coming up the road. There's always about forty foxhounds and they mill about outside the pub and mix with the people.' She laughed. 'Lulu came the last time. Boxing Day morning. She thought she'd died and gone to Heaven.'

'Boxing Day morning,' Jimmy said. 'My people have a party at home on Christmas night. They don't get up until lunchtime next day. Although Arthur does if there's a football match.' He smiled down at her. 'We come from different worlds, Ria.'

'Does it matter?' she asked.

'Not to me,' Jimmy said and she nestled closer to him.

The church clock chimed and Ria sat upright. The ducklings were sailing behind their mother in a perfect V formation, like a squadron in flight, on the still tranquil river. But there was no sign of Paddy and Lulu, and Ria knew there would be search parties out looking for her if she didn't go home.

The sky was clouded over now but they were not dark clouds. The sun was still visible, a white blur trying to break through.

'Jimmy,' she said quietly. 'I have to go.'

Jimmy nodded.

'I've had a lovely day' she said. 'I didn't want it to end – ever. It's so lovely here. And being with you...' Her voice trailed.

Parish Field,' Jimmy said fondly. 'We'll come again.'

'Will we?' she asked plaintively.

'Sure we will,' he said.

But they never did.

CHAPTER FIVE

The next Wednesday afternoon Jimmy waited in the bushes until he saw Charlie Spence's van go hurtling by and down the lane towards the village. Then he went over to the wire fence and barked a couple of times. Rambo was the first to appear.

'Hey, Jimmy!' he called in greeting

'Just thought I'd say hello,' Jimmy said. 'How are you doing?'

'Oh, I'm all right, I suppose,' Rambo said. 'It's Rocky. He's really fed up.'

'Why? What's happened?'

Rocky overheard this as he came ambling up to the wire.

'That's it,' he said. '*Nothing's* happened. Nothing ever happens. We have absolutely nothing to do. And it's boring.'

'We never have anything to do,' Rambo said.

'No,' Rocky conceded. 'But it's different now. I mean, we know now that dogs can go out and meet people, make friends, have fun. Like last week when we met that little lad. We shouldn't be stuck in here all day working for that idiot Spence.' To Jimmy he said, 'You showed us things can be different.'

Jimmy nodded. 'So it's my fault, is it? I shouldn't have got you interested in Bobbie.'

'No, no,' Rocky said. 'That was great.'

'Well, I'll tell you what,' Jimmy said. 'If you've got some free time, why don't we watch a movie?'

'A movie?' they said.

'Yeah. What's your favourite film?'

'Favourite film?' Rambo said. 'We don't have a favourite film.'

'We've never watched a film,' Rocky admitted.

'Really?' Jimmy was surprised but then he remembered they didn't live in a house. They lived in kennels.

'Listen,' he said, 'you've got a couple of hours, haven't you?'

'Sure,' Rocky said. 'Spence has only just gone out.'

'Well, you come with me and we'll go and watch a good movie. I promise you, you'll love it.'

'Where?' Rocky asked. 'Where would we go?'

'We'll go to my house,' Jimmy said. 'Folks are out at work. We can watch a film on television.'

The Rottweilers looked at each other. 'Yeah!' they said together. 'Let's go.'

Jimmy eyed them critically, as if mentally measuring them. 'Yes,' he said, after a moment. 'I think you can squeeze through.'

The house where Jimmy lived backed on to a field and hc usually came home that way. The next door neighbour was used to seeing him jump on to the dustbin and deftly ease his way in through the unlatched window. He crouched down by the fence, made sure the neighbour was not around, then signalled to the others to follow. Up he went and in through the window. Holding the window open with a paw now, he called to Rocky who was first in line, 'Come on, Rock, you'll get through all right.'

Rocky leapt on to the dustbin and in through the window. It was a tight squeeze but he made it easily enough.

'Come on,' Jimmy called to Rambo. 'Straight through.'

Rambo hesitated, jumped on the dustbin and fell off.

Jimmy looked out of the window. 'Sh!' he warned. Then in a loud whisper, 'Are you all right?'

Rambo nodded, waited a moment then tried again, this time with such force that he crashed through the open window and fell to the outhouse floor taking the other two with him.

'No problem,' he said, proud of himself.

'Clumsy oaf!' Rocky called him.

'He's all right, aren't you, Rambo?' Jimmy said. 'No harm done. Now follow me and be careful. Don't make any mess or I'll be in trouble.'

Rocky looked hard at Rambo. 'No mess. Okay?'

Jimmy led the way into the living room and told them to sit down in front of a very large television screen. It was a smallish room and the television screen seemed far too big, out of all proportion to the rest of the furniture.

To some people, Jimmy said, a little embarrassed and feeling thc need to explain, the size of their television screen is important. It's a kind of status symbol. The bigger the better.

The television was always on stand-by and Jimmy knew how to operate the remote control. His owner liked to watch and record films for his collection, though he never seemed to watch them again once he had recorded and stored them.

Jimmy looked down the list of available titles – *Shrek, Forrest Gump, The Jungle Book* and more – before making his choice.

'Hey! You two are going to love this. It's called *The Jungle Book*.'

Rocky and Rambo looked at each other blankly then they watched, open-mouthed, as the titles came up. At once they were transfixed, loving every moment. They loved Mowgli and they loved Balou and they rocked with laughter every time the snake was tied in knots. Then, when King Louis came on with his groovy singing and crazy dancing, they couldn't contain themselves and they just *had* to join in.

'Sh!' Jimmy warned them. 'Someone might hear us and we're not supposed to be in here.'

'Again!' Rambo cried as it came to an end. 'I want to see it again.'

'Yeah!' Rocky agreed. 'Fantastic!'

'I don't think there's time,' Jimmy told them gently. 'We have to get out of here before the missus comes home. And what about your boss? You'd better be there when he gets back.'

'*Boop-de-do*,' sang Rambo

And Rocky joined in with, '*I wanna be like you-hoo*.'

'All right, all right,' Jimmy said with a laugh. 'We can come back and watch it again another day. We have to get out of here fast and without anyone seeing us. Okay?'

He switched off the television and obediently they followed him through the kitchen into the outhouse. One by one they dropped down into the garden, then they left by the way they came.

Jimmy walked back with them across the field towards Edgecroft and as far as the end of the lane leading to Spence's place. And again he laughed as he watched them go up the lane, dancing like Mowgli and Balou, and singing 'I wanna be like you-hoo'.

A week later the weather was fine and the village green was ablaze with daffodils and hyacinths. The crocuses and tulips were about to bloom and Jimmy's step was light and carefree.

His instructions were to bring the Rottweilers to the concert by the river. Everyone had been told they must make them welcome and most members of the gang looked forward to their arrival with interest. But when he got to the wire at Charlie Spence's place, Jimmy found that Rocky and Rambo were clearly not happy.

'What's going on?' he asked.

'It's him,' Rambo said, meaning Rocky. 'He reckons we shouldn't come out any more.'

'It's *too* dangerous,' Rocky insisted. 'The man is mad, completely and utterly mad. A psychopath!'

'Spence?' Jimmy asked.

'Who else? When we got back here last Wednesday he was back, wasn't he? Came home early. I expect he's been banned from the Bull now and he has nowhere else to go.'

'Yeah,' Rambo said. 'He had two big crates of beer in the van.'

'He went completely mad...' Rocky went on.

'Bonkers,' Rambo confirmed.

'... when he found we were missing. And when we did come in under the wire, he was waiting in the bushes. He had this strap, a thick leather thing with metal studs and he really laid into us.'

'I wanted to tear him apart,' Rambo said.

'So did I,' Rocky said. 'We could have finished him off there and then if we'd wanted to.'

'And I wanted to,' Rambo said.

'Yeah,' Rocky agreed, 'but we couldn't do that, could we? They would have come looking for us. They would have caught us and had us put down. No doubt about that.'

'It would have been worth it,' Rambo said.

'No,' Jimmy said. 'Rocky is right. We'll have to think of a better way to deal with *Mister* Spence.'

He wasn't sure what to do. He had planned to invite them to the concert. He knew they would enjoy it. There were more volunteers than usual because the circus would be coming through the village soon and there was a dog called Rex who reckoned he was a scout, always looking for new talent. He held what he claimed were genuine auditions for jobs with the circus but Jimmy was not entirely convinced.

This dog Rex was full of himself and he called the show he produced 'The Rex-factor', but Jimmy had noticed that nobody was ever offered a job with the circus as a result of winning one of these competitions. And, anyway, this Rex seemed to be mainly interested in the bitches.

Jimmy decided the concert was not important. If the Rottweilers were not coming out this might be his opportunity to get inside the place and take a look at the pit bulls.

'Listen,' he said seriously, 'if Spence lays into you two with a strap, what might he be doing to those poor young pit bulls?'

The Rottweilers looked at each other. 'We don't know what he might be doing,' Rocky said. 'We haven't seen much of them. In fact, we haven't seen them at all.'

'That's right,' Rambo agreed.

'We saw them when they first arrived,' Rocky said, 'but he keeps them out of sight. He never lets them out of the sheds.'

He pointed to three sheds, one fairly large, the other two quite small. 'We're not allowed over there.'

The sheds had no windows and from where the three dogs were standing they couldn't see any doors. The doors were at the far ends. The big shed was the nearest to the lane and Jimmy guessed this must be the place where Ria and her owner heard the pit bulls cry when they were being beaten.

'So what's he got in there?' Jimmy asked. 'Just the two pups?'

'No,' Rambo said. 'Six more little ones turned up last week.'

'He keeps the new ones in that first shed,' Rocky said, 'and the other two in the next one.'

'What about the big shed?'

'I reckon that's where he does the training.'

Jimmy looked around. Spring had arrived and most people in Warkwood were beginning to tidy up their gardens ready for what promised to be a long hot summer. Spence's garden was a mess. Tired-looking bushes, worn-out lawn. Assorted debris scattered from overflowing bins. Evidence of misuse and neglect all around.

And the bungalow where he lived! Flaking woodwork sorely in need of a coat of paint. Grimy windows long unwashed. Rusting drains and a broken gutter hanging loose.

'Can I come in?' he asked.

Rocky hesitated. 'I dunno. If he's been banned from the Bull he might be back early. He has nowhere else to go.'

'Nobody else will have him,' Rambo said with a guffaw.

'Well, if he does come back I'll just have to hide until it's safe to leave,' Jimmy said, then softly, 'I'd really like to take a look at the pit bulls, see if they're okay. If you don't mind, that is.'

Rocky was feeling a bit embarrassed, realising he and Rambo ought to have been more protective. The two pit bulls were just tiny puppies when they first arrived. Now he had no idea what Spence might have turned them into. 'Yeah, sure,' he said. 'Why not. Let's all take a look.'

'He filled up the hole under the fence,' Rambo said. 'He put a big flagstone over the place where we used to get out.'

'That's all right,' Rocky said. 'No problem. We can dig another hole.' To Jimmy he said, 'We'll dig this side, you dig that.'

They moved along the high wire fence until Rocky chose a spot that was hidden behind a bank of conifers. There was not much space between the trees and the wire, but Rocky and Rambo took it in turns to scoop out and soon a small mound of soil appeared. Jimmy's progress was much slower, but he stuck to the task and soon he, too, had his small mound of earth.

It was tiring work but the pace quickened when it was clear they were close to a breakthrough. Then, as Rambo attacked the hole on one side, Jimmy on the other, the dividing wall collapsed and they scooped out the soil until their paws met.

'Yeah!' Rambo cried in triumph.

Rocky took over now, making the hole wider, and soon Jimmy was able to squeeze through. They waited, all three with their ears cocked, listening for the sound of a van. But all was quiet.

'Great!' Jimmy said. 'Let's go.'

CHAPTER SIX

It was still very quiet. The only vehicles that came this way, they knew, were coming to Spence's place because a few yards further on the lane petered out and became no more than a footpath.

Rocky led them swiftly across the potholed driveway, past the rusted remains of an abandoned motorcycle, a solidified bag of cement and other discarded rubbish, where they sought the cover of the three sheds.

'I bet the doors are locked,' Jimmy said.

'I don't think so,' Rocky said. 'We're supposed to be the locks that keep people out.'

He was right. The first shed had just a latch. He lifted the latch, opened the door only slightly and looked inside. Jimmy stood back as Rambo jostled to take a look. Then Rocky pushed open the door and signalled for them to follow.

Six tiny pit bull puppies were lying in a basket. Most had their pink and watery eyes closed or barely open, but one raised its head and looked directly at the intruders.

Rocky went forward slowly. 'Hello, puppies,' he said gently. 'Are you all right? Is he feeding you properly?'

The wide-awake one stared at him blankly. Of course, he or she hadn't learned to speak yet but the little pup didn't seem afraid in any way. Rocky sat down close by and murmured softly in the little pup's ear and the pup responded by leaning into him.

Jimmy was impressed by Rocky's gentle, caring manner. Rambo knelt close to the others now and prodded one gently with his nose. The little pup, eyes half closed, didn't recoil. It simply inclined its head towards Rambo in a gesture of total trust.

Rambo seemed surprised. 'They're not scared of us, are they?'

'Why would they be?' Rocky answered. 'They haven't had their brains poisoned yet by Spence.'

Jimmy was more than encouraged by the way the Rottweilers were behaving. He knew now he had won them over.

'We need to get these little ones to a place of safety,' he said. 'But not yet. First of all we must see what's going on next door.'

Rocky and Rambo were reluctant to leave the pups, but Jimmy insisted there was no time to lose. 'Spence could come back at any moment,' he said.

'Love you,' Rambo called to the uncomprehending pups and the trio trooped out, closing the door carefully behind them.

They had no idea what they might find in the next shed as, cautiously, Rocky lifted the latch. The two older pit bulls, bigger and stronger though not yet fully grown, seemed to cower back, perhaps expecting Spence. But when they saw the three dogs they reacted ferociously.

Locked in separate cages, they hurled themselves forward as if determined to break out and tear into the first dog they met. But as Jimmy and the Rottweilers approached, clearly unafraid, they calmed down a little.

'What's up with you two?' Rambo asked aggressively. 'I could eat the pair of you for breakfast.'

'No, no, Rambo,' Jimmy said quietly. 'That's not the way.'

'Well, who do they think they are?'

'Cool it, Ram,' Rocky said. 'That's how they've been brought up to behave. Spence is turning them into crazy fighters.'

The two pit bulls were seething, almost foaming at the mouth in frustration, wanting to spring but knowing they were caged.

'Let Jimmy talk to them,' he added.

Jimmy nodded and the Rottweilers drew back. He went forward and calmly crouched low, close to both cages. 'You two look pretty tough,' he said, in a friendly way. 'I bet you could beat most dogs.'

They glanced at each other and he was not sure they understood what he was saying. 'But we haven't come here to fight,' he went on. 'We're your friends. We've come to set you free.'

He looked at them closely and was shocked by what he saw. One had a four inch gash, an untreated and still open neck wound, the other had a torn ear and both had numerous scars and bruises.

'Can you understand what I'm saying?' he asked gently.

They looked at each other, their noses quivering, their teeth bared. Then one nodded.

'Good,' Jimmy said. 'What about you?'

Still hostile, the other one nodded.

'You know Charlie Spence? The man who owns you? The man who is supposed to take care of you and feed you properly?'

'He doesn't feed us,' the first one said. 'He gives us scraps, then when he feels like it he throws some food down over there...' He nodded towards a sawdusted area in the wide shed. '... we have to fight each other for it.'

'And sometimes you're very hungry,' Jimmy said, 'so you fight.'

They both nodded.

'Well, look,' he told them, 'this is all wrong. You are not fighting dogs. There is no such thing as a fighting dog. Fighting dogs are what bad men turn good dogs into. They make you fight each other. They make it so that you have to fight or starve. Then when you think that's the only way you can live you are ready to fight any dog, any time, any place. And that's what they want.'

'But why?' the one with the four inch wound asked.

'Because when you're fully grown and they reckon you're ready, they put you into dogfights for money. They put you in a ring with someone else's dog, a dog that's been trained to kill as you will be. But you are not killers. No dog is a killer. It's what evil men like Charlie Spence turn you into.'

The two dogs were very quiet, a little ashamed as they glanced at each other. They didn't want to fight. They had both had enough. Yet it was fight or starve.

'There's nothing for you here,' Jimmy went on. 'You may become good fighters, champions even, and you might make lots of money for your so-called trainer. But it'll kill you. You'll either die in the pit or you'll be so badly hurt that you have to be put down.'

'So what are you saying?' one asked with a frown.

'I'm saying we can help,' Jimmy told him. 'That's why we're here. What's happening with you is wrong. You should be part of a happy family where they take care of you, feed you properly and love you. Most people love their dogs. Most men and women are nice to us and little kids, why, they're crazy about us. They love us and we love them back. There's no way you could love a man like Charlie Spence.'

Rocky and Rambo were listening to this. They looked at each other now. This was what *they* wanted, too. A family of their own. Maybe with some little kid like that Bobbie who they could love and protect.

'We're going to help here,' Rocky said suddenly. 'That's a promise.'

The two young pit bulls were much calmer now, as if soothed by Jimmy's quietly reassuring words, and eager to hear more.

'We have a lot of friends,' Jimmy said. 'A gang of dogs, all breeds, and they'll all help. What we'll do is work out a plan, set something up. I'll see our leader, find a way to get you out of here then, when you're free, we'll take you to a place where you'll be safe. Agreed?'

Again the two pit bulls looked at each other.

'It means no more fights,' Jimmy promised. 'You will have to work together. You will have to trust us and come with us when we come for you. And we'll see that you get good food and a place to stay.'

'But when?' one asked. 'I mean, Spence will want us to fight next time he brings the food in. If we don't fight we don't eat.'

'More than that,' the other said. 'If he thinks we're refusing to fight he lays into us with a big strap.'

'If we hear you howling we'll come for you and we'll lay into *him*,' Rocky threatened.

'Yeah,' Rambo agreed enthusiastically.

'No,' Jimmy said. 'You know you mustn't do that. This has to be thought out carefully and it will be.'

The pit bulls were nodding hopefully. 'The sooner the better?' one asked.

'Yes,' Jimmy told him. 'Now are you two friends? Good mates? You will stick together, no matter what?'

Again they looked at each other and this time they nodded.

'Promise?' Jimmy said.

'Promise,' one said.

'Promise,' said the other.

It was quiet in the copse, the April sun filtering down through fresh yellowish leaves still wet with recent rain. Don Schnauzer, Chalkie the Scot and The Professor listened carefully to Jimmy's detailed report. He told them how the two young pit bulls were forced to fight each other for basic food, how they had inflicted dreadful injuries on each other and how he had been sickened by the sight of the torn ear and the open unattended gash of a wound. They were being groomed to take part in illegal dogfights, he said, where they have to fight for prize money and where gangs of men lay bets on which dog will survive.

'Survive?' Chalkie asked uneasily.

'It's often a fight to the death,' Jimmy told him.

'Dogfighting has been going on for centuries,' The Professor said. 'Throughout history many countries have tried to put a stop to it but without success. It keeps coming back like an unpleasant rash. It was going on at the Colosseum in Roman times and it's going on now right across the world. Australia, America, the Far East and in many parts of Europe, including here in Britain.'

'One of these young pit bulls looks worse than the other,' Jimmy said. 'You know, more seriously injured. What if he gets so badly beaten up he can't fight?'

'They would use him as bait. They would throw him in the pit and let the fighting dog loose to tear him apart before the real fight starts. They call dogs they use like that "bait". But they don't just use dogs. They use cats or rabbits, sometimes *wild* animals, anything they can get their hands on.'

'But what if this young pit bull realises he's fighting for his life,' Chalkie said, 'and he fights back? He could do some real damage to their precious prize fighter.'

'No,' The Professor said. 'They don't allow that to happen. If it's a dog that has not been considered quite good enough they will tape up his snout so tight that he can't do any damage to their star attraction.'

'It's no very sporting,' Chalkie said.

'They call it a sport but it's not a sport. It's a mindless orgy of despicable violence enjoyed by criminals.'

'They are not human,' Don Schnauzer said. 'What they do is *in*human. And it's happening here, in our village, and we are not going to tolerate it.' He looked at Jimmy and nodded solemnly in appreciation. 'You have done a fine job, Jimmy, to get this far. Our priority now must be to rescue the pit bulls and somehow save the puppies, too.'

'That will not be easy, Dogfather,' Jimmy said. 'The puppies are no more than babies. They are not yet able to walk.'

'We must devise a plan,' The Professor said.

'You are sure the Rottweilers are willing to help? Not going to change their minds at the last minute?'

'I don't think so, Dogfather,' Jimmy told him. 'They realise now that there are better things to do than work for Charlie Spence. I believe they genuinely want to get away from there. They would really like to be part of a good family. I'm sure they won't let us down.'

'Then we will hold a special meeting of the Council and I would like you, Jimmy, to be present.'

Jimmy bowed. 'This is indeed an honour, Dogfather.'

'And one that you deserve,' The Professor said.

Jimmy walked back to the village with Chalkie, consciously slowing down for Chalkie to keep up.

'I reckon the Chief is going to invite ye to join the Council permanently, Jim,' Chalkie said, already out of breath.

But Jimmy was barely listening. His main concern just then was how soon they could do something about the pit bulls and rescue those six little puppies.

'An' ye should be proud o' that,' Chalkie told him.

'What?' Jimmy said. 'Oh, yeah, sure. But I'd like to get things moving, Chalkie. We must do something before Spence does.'

'But ye *would* like to join the Council, would ye no?'

'Well...' Jimmy hesitated. 'Yes, but I don't know if I'm up to it. The Don and The Professor, they're so clever. They know such a lot about so many things.'

Chalkie laughed. 'What about me? I'm on the Council.'

'That's what I mean. You know lots, too. You all do.'

'And so will you.'

'But take The Professor. I mean, how does he know all that stuff about dogfighting. And what he said about this dog*baiting*. Where does he get all his information?'

'Och, that's easy. He goes on the computer. He gets what he wants to know from websites like Wikipedia.'

'Wiki what?'

'It's like an encyclopaedia on the Internet. Ye can find almost anything ye want to know on there. Great for research. It's not always accurate or even true sometimes. But most of the time it is and there are plenty of other websites to double check.'

Jimmy's people had a computer but they didn't seem to use it much. Doreen didn't use it at all but sometimes, when she was out or she had gone to bed, Arthur would use it to place bets on horses and football matches. Who would score the first goal and that sort of thing.

'I could never use a computer,' he said sadly. 'It looks far too complicated to me.'

'Of course ye could,' Chalkie assured him. 'Ye watch television, don't ye? Ye know how to switch the television on when no one's in. Well, ye would soon learn how to switch the computer on. And once it's on ye can work out how to use it. It's not difficult.

And anyway, I could teach ye.'

'So you know how to use a computer?'

'I do, yes. But I've had to learn. And I've done quite a bit now. The trouble is, my man has a laptop. I find if it's closed I can't always get it open. If he goes out and leaves it open I'll go on it right away. But he doesn't do that very often. Most of the time he switches it off and waits for the screen to go blank before he puts the top down. Sometimes though he forgets and goes off to bed leaving it open. I have all night then to do whatever I want and it's great. A computer can open up the whole world.'

'How do you mean?'

'I can chat on-line to people all over the world.'

'People all over the world *talk* to you?'

'They send messages on the screen and I send messages back.'

'Why would people send messages to a dog?'

'They don't *know* I'm a dog, do they?'

Jimmy was nodding now, seeing the possibilities. 'Our computer doesn't have a lid.'

'Well then, ye shouldn'y have any problem. If someone comes in when you're on-line ye pretend to be asleep. They'll just think they must have left it on.'

'Could I send messages to, say, Ria?'

'Of course, as long as she has access to a computer and knows how to use it. Ye could talk to her on Facebook.'

'Facebook?'

Chalkie came to a halt and sat down in the long grass. 'Come here,' he said. 'Sit down and I'll explain. How long have ye got?'

CHAPTER SEVEN

The Council held their meeting. The plan was discussed in full, agreed and put to the members. Every member, it was explained, would have a part to play. Of course, the only day the plan could be carried out was a Wednesday when Charlie Spence went down to the village, a Wednesday afternoon, as soon as possible. There were several jobs to be allocated, the Dogfather announced and he allowed The Professor to explain.

'First of all,' The Professor said, 'a small means of transport must be acquired.'

'That lets me out,' Ringo murmured softly. 'I can't drive.'

'Not a motor car, you idiot,' Paddy whispered. 'I think it's some sort of buggy they want.'

The Professor looked around sternly to command attention. 'There are six tiny pups to be rescued,' he continued. 'They are too small to run. They can't walk, in fact. So they must be transported safely in some way from this shed on Spence's smallholding to the vet's surgery in the village. The best of the suggestions we have had so far is a trolley from a supermarket.'

'A trolley from a supermarket?' Rhavi queried. 'The nearest supermarket is in Bramble and that's over two miles away.'

'Doesn't your Ali have any trolleys?' someone asked.

'Of course not,' Rhavi said. 'We're a minimarket. We only stock essentials.'

'Perhaps Ali should open a supermarket,' Ringo suggested, 'save people having to go all that way.'

'Ringo,' Chalkie said in exasperation. 'Shut up.'

'The plan is,' The Professor went on, 'that three of us should go to the supermarket in Bramble the night before the rescue, find a trolley in the supermarket car park, the smallest trolley we can find and bring it back here. Well, not here exactly. We would probably need to hide it somewhere near Edgecroft Lane.'

'And how will we do that?' Paddy asked.

'Well,' The Professor told him, 'this is where brains and real ingenuity come in and you, Paddy, have both in abundance. I propose, gentlemen, that Paddy and two others are asked to carry out the very important task of finding and delivering a suitable supermarket trolley.'

'I second that,' Chalkie said.

'All agreed?' The Professor asked and everyone, except Paddy, nodded in agreement.

'Agreed.' Don Schnauzer confirmed.

'Me and my big mouth,' Paddy said ruefully.

'Now,' The Professor announced, 'apparently, we have a way to get into Spence's place but getting out might not be easy. The way in, I'm afraid, is rather restricted. It's by way of a hole under the wire netting fence. This means we can only get in one by one and, of course, more importantly, we can only get out one by one.'

'Can't we make the hole bigger?' someone asked.

'There's the danger of discovery,' The Professor answered. 'The element of surprise is paramount in a venture such as this.'

'I'm working on that, Professor,' Jimmy told him. 'I'm hoping to find a better way in.'

The Professor nodded. 'Now you may not all know this, but our main helpers in this somewhat dangerous enterprise are two large and, I understand, rather fearsome-looking Rottweilers.'

There were murmurs among the assembled dogs and speculative glances all round. Rottweilers? How scary is that?

'No, no, Professor,' Jimmy spoke up. 'There's no need for us to be afraid of these Rottweilers. They are on our side and, after all, they are just dogs like us. They hate Charlie Spence as much as we do, probably more so, and anyway, without their help we have no hope of succeeding. Believe me, they are with us all the way.'

'Do you actually know them?' Rhavi asked. 'I mean, *personally*. Have you met them yourself?'

'Of course,' Jimmy said. 'They're my friends.'

The Dogfather held up a paw. 'Be assured, brothers, Jimmy has met with them several times. He assures me they are with us. I am happy to take Jimmy's word for it and so should you be.'

Jimmy gulped, hoping Rocky and Rambo would not let him down.

'Jimmy will see them,' Don Schnauzer said, 'and make sure they fully understand our plan. On Wednesday we must all be prepared.'

Ringo barked politely. 'Dogfather,' he said, 'when we do get inside Spence's place, what do we have to do?'

Don Schnauzer looked at Jimmy. 'Jimmy?'

'The pit bulls are housed in two sheds,' Jimmy told them. 'In the first shed there are six very young pups. In the second shed, the two young pit bulls.'

'Are they safe?' Max the German shepherd asked, meaning the two young pit bulls. 'If they've been trained as fighting dogs they might be a little crazy. They may not want to come with us. And if they don't want to come, believe me, they won't.'

All these questions were unnerving Jimmy. 'Look,' he said with a confidence he didn't feel. 'They *do* want to come. I'm sure there'll be no trouble. They're expecting us. They *want* to get out of there. And the sooner the better, they say.'

'Good,' Max said. 'I'm getting a bit too old for prize fighting.'

Don Schnauzer looked to The Professor to restore confidence. 'In the meantime,' The Professor announced, 'Max and I will visit as many of our neighbouring villages as we can, even go into Bramble. We will talk to the local dogs and, we hope, win their support. We want as many of them as possible to come to Warkwood and converge on Edgecroft Lane next Wednesday afternoon at three o'clock. We will ask them to lie in wait in the long grass along the lane. If Spence's van arrives, at a signal from us, they will all come out and flood the lane, block his progress.'

'Knowing Charlie Spence,' Jimmy said, only half seriously, 'he might drive right through them.'

'He wouldn't dare,' Rhavi said. 'Just think of the trouble he'd be in. He only gets away with what he does because he keeps it all very private. Last thing he wants is publicity.'

'Very true,' The Professor said. 'So, are we ready for action?'

Heads were nodding, tails wagging in anticipation.

'An' what will be the timetable to all this?' Paddy asked.

'First, we need to have the trolley in place, somewhere close to the entrance to Spence's smallholding. Ringo will ensure the dogs we recruit are lying in wait along the lane by three thirty. Then, as soon as Spence's van leaves to go to the village, Ringo will give us his usual three barks. We enter the property by the best means available, find the pups, bring them out one by one and put them in the trolley. Then we get the young pit bulls and we take them all down to the village vet. Mr Hill the vet will wonder what's going on, but when he sees the wounds on the two pit bulls he will feel obliged to treat them.'

'The two pit bulls might just run off,' Rhavi said. 'You know what these youngsters are like. They never do as they're told.'

'No,' The Professor said confidently. 'Jimmy has made them promise they will come with us. He has promised them their wounds will be treated and they will be well taken care of. They shouldn't give us any trouble.'

The Professor raised his head and addressed the assembled members. 'If there are any further questions Jimmy and I will do our best to answer them.'

The Dogfather indicated he wished to speak now and at once the group fell silent. 'Brothers,' he said quietly, 'this is a difficult but extremely important undertaking, probably the most important mission we have been called upon to carry out. It is simply a battle between what is right and what is wrong. We are in the right. Let us make sure we win.'

The audience of dogs nodded and barked enthusiastically and the meeting came to an end.

It was a bright moonlit night in early April. Stars sparkled like diamonds against a black sky. Paddy and Ringo waited for the village store to close. Then, at the stroke of eleven on the church clock, the shutters came down, the lights in the store went out and after several minutes Rhavi appeared.

He had waited as usual for Ali's pat on the head and words of endearment before stretching out in his basket as if tired and ready for bed. But as soon as Ali and Mrs Ali went upstairs and he heard the door to the bedroom close, he went into action.

Quietly lifting the latch on the cellar door he went down into the darkness. The store was at the end of a row of old houses and, like the houses, the store had a cellar into which, in the old days, the coalman would empty his bags of coal. But since those days central heating had been installed, the last remnants of coal had been cleared away and the cellar had been thoroughly cleaned and whitewashed. It was used now as a stock room.

The grid and the hole down which the coalman used to empty

his coal was still there and it was not difficult for a small child or a dog to wriggle up the short narrow channel, move the grid aside and climb out into the street. And that was what Rhavi did, as he had on many occasions.

Without a word he fell in beside Paddy and Ringo and together they set off with grim resolve, heads down and teeth gritted, as if they were going into battle. But the mood didn't last. They were only going to steal a supermarket trolley. Or perhaps only *borrow* one. Don Schnauzer would probably make them take it back when they had finished with it. And anyway, the grim resolve would have been difficult to sustain all the way to Bramble – especially with Ringo fooling about.

Now they had a decision to make. Where they left the village the road diverged. To the right was the main road. To the left was an unmade road, little more than a footpath in parts, that ran beside the river.

'Best way is up the highway,' Ringo said. 'It's more on a level.'

'We already worked that out,' Rhavi told him. 'But how we are going to drag a shopping trolley all the way back to the village without being seen I have no idea.'

'If we go this way,' Paddy said, indicating the main road, 'it will be quicker, so it will. Then we can come back by the river. It'll be downhill part of the way and that hill must be at least a half mile long.'

'We can't just push it down the hill,' Rhavi argued. 'It might end up in the river. Then where would we be?'

'Up the creek without a trolley,' Ringo said.

There was little traffic about and it was quiet along the highway. The night air was fresh and it was pleasant enough and they made good progress. And it was not long before they saw the shadowy huddle of the town ahead.

Against a dark blue sky lay the black outline of a sleeping Bramble. Here and there, like a playing card in the distance, a solitary window light stood out and occasionally, as they approached, the sweeping headlights of a car sliced through the darkness.

'Sure an' everyone's in their beds,' Paddy said.

They had talked and talked all the way, mostly rubbish, but now, mindful of the job ahead, all three fell silent. At least, Paddy and Rhavi did. Ringo was suddenly excited as he saw his panting breath was clearly visible on the colder night air.

'Hey!' he cried. He put his head to his raised paw then blew out some air. 'Look at me! I'm smoking a cigarette.'

'And why would anybody want to do *that*?,' Rhavi said. 'Grow up, Ringo.'

A car sped by on the dual carriageway, picking out the line of studs down the centre of the road.

'Look at that!' Ringo said, intrigued. 'Those things light up when a car goes by.'

'They're cats' eyes,' Rhavi said.

'What? You're joking.'

'It's true,' Paddy told him. 'That's what they do around here, so it is. They catch all the stray cats, take out their eyes and stick them down the centre of the road. That way they light up when a car passes by and the driver can tell if he's on the right side of the road.'

'You're having me on,' Ringo said. 'The cats would soon get wise to that. They'd never catch 'em.'

'It's true,' Paddy said. 'They have these enormous fishing nets, so they do.'

Ringo looked concerned. 'Bit rough on the cats. I mean, I don't like cats but...'

'Ringo,' Rhavi said, 'shut up. And you stop it, Paddy. We have work to do.'

'I'm not exactly sure where this supermarket is,' Paddy told him. 'I've never actually been there.'

'No problem,' Rhavi said. 'I've been a few times in the van with Ali when he goes to stock up. I've never been inside though. Dogs are not allowed in.'

'Ali stocks up at the supermarket?' Ringo queried.

'No,' Rhavi said defensively. 'He sometimes buys things there when people ask for something we don't stock.'

'I bet he could buy all his stuff there,' Ringo said, 'and still make a profit. The supermarket's much cheaper than him.'

'Is that it?' Paddy asked, pointing to a long line of shops, all of them closed and in darkness. At one end was the supermarket, with a couple of vans parked at the side

'Yeah, that's it,' Rhavi said. 'Let's go'

The car park was dark but as they approached, with a bright moon high above, it was not difficult to see there was a problem. The supermarket trolleys were linked together in four long lines, locked in place by chains that ran through them from end to end.

Paddy and Rhavi looked at each other. The trolleys were all of the deep variety. There didn't seem to be any of the shallow ones about. They tried to release one at the end of the line but they were all locked firmly in place.

Ringo took one look at the chained trolleys and went off on a speculative search for a loose one.

'We'll have to look around the car park for one they've missed or try down there,' Rhavi said, pointing his nose towards a dark street. 'Some people are awful, you know, very inconsiderate. They take a trolley to their car parked out on the street and they don't bring it back. They just leave it there.'

'Why don't they put their cars in the car park?' Paddy asked.

'Perhaps the car parks get full.'

Paddy nodded and followed Rhavi towards the street, but he was not optimistic. It was beginning to look as if their long tiring hike had been in vain, but then they were halted by a rattling sound as Ringo came round a corner on his hind legs, pushing a shallow trolley ahead of him.

'Is this what you're looking for?' he asked with a big grin.

'Where did you get it?' Rhavi asked.

'Someone left it in a doorway down the side of the store.'

'Ringo,' Paddy said, 'I could kiss you, so I could.'

'Gerroff!' Ringo said and, with their spirits raised, all three began to steer the trolley across the car park towards the unmade road that ran downhill to the riverside.

As soon as they came to where the shadowy road began, Ringo climbed up into the trolley and stretched out in comfort. 'I found it,' he declared, 'so you two can give me a ride.'

Rhavi and Paddy looked at each other. It was typical Ringo. As far as he was concerned, he'd done his bit.

'Better hold tight then,' Rhavi said. 'It might suddenly take off.'

They started home, singing softly as they went, but soon the road began to dip and become much steeper. Rhavi and Paddy had to run to keep up with the trolley. Ringo, who had been lying back, watching the stars, suddenly realised the trolley was gathering speed.

'Hey!' he cried, sitting up. 'What's happening?'

The trolley went faster and faster as it careered downhill and there was nothing either Rhavi or Paddy could do to slow it down. Ringo tried to stand up, ready to jump off before it hit something, but the trolley was going faster and faster and he kept falling back.

'Jump!' Rhavi cried as he and Paddy ran with the trolley, unable to stop it or even slow it down. 'Jump out!'

A man who had spent most of the evening in the Black Bull was staggering up the hill towards them on his way home. He came to a halt and stepped aside, swaying back and forth, his glazed eyes blinking at the strange spectacle before him.

Two dogs were barking madly as they hurtled downhill alongside a trolley from the supermarket. A *third* dog was actually *in* the trolley, clinging on as if he feared he was about to be thrown out.

The man scratched his head, wondering as he went unsteadily on his way just how many drinks he'd had.

CHAPTER EIGHT

Jimmy decided it was time he called on Ria. He felt he ought to keep her informed and, anyway, he liked talking to her, sitting on the grass verge outside the large detached house where she lived, even if a garden wall did separate them. But when he passed by, hoping she would be around, he found she was not alone. Lulu was with her.

'Hi, you two!' he said pleasantly. 'I'm sorry I haven't been in touch. Things have been pretty hectic, but it's all set up now. We each have a job to do and we're ready to go.'

'Aren't you lucky?' Lulu said.

'What about us?' Ria asked. 'We don't have a job.

'Well, y'know,' Jimmy said apologetically, 'it's mainly a job for dogs.'

'Oh, is it?' Lulu demanded. 'You saying we're useless or something?'

'No, no,' Jimmy said. 'Of course not.'

'We started all this, Jimmy,' Ria said quietly. 'We should be allowed to play our part.'

'You tell that what's-his-name,' Lulu said. 'Top dog?'

'The Dogfather,' Jimmy said.

'You tell him he'd better count us in.'

Jimmy didn't know what to say. He couldn't think of anything just then. He was preoccupied with looking into Ria's eyes.

'It's all set up, is it?' she asked. 'So what's going to happen?'

'Wednesday,' Jimmy said. 'Wednesday afternoon when Charlie Spence goes down to the village we are going to rescue the pit bulls. Not just the two he's training. He has six little pups, too, and we're going to rescue them all.'

'And how are you going to do that?'

'You've seen the place, Ria. You know what it's like. We're going to have to get under the wire and bring them out.'

'What about his guard dogs, the Rottweilers?'

'They are on our side.'

'Are you sure of that?'

'Yes,' Jimmy said, though he was still not absolutely certain Rocky and Rambo would remain loyal when the time came. 'They are all right. They are tired of working for Spence.'

'They could just run away,' Lulu said.

'Yes,' Jimmy said, 'but when they saw what was happening to the pit bulls they wanted to help. The poor things have got some terrible wounds and we need to get them to the village vet.'

'Well,' Lulu said. 'I hope they *do* want to help. You know what Rottweilers are like. Vicious thugs.'

'No, they're not!' Jimmy told her vehemently. 'And that's not worthy of you, Lulu. They're just dogs, no better, no worse than pit bulls and you defended pit bulls when someone said they were vicious. Rottweilers just have a bad reputation, that's all. And anyway, these two are my friends. They've been to my house to watch a movie. They don't live in Spence's bungalow. He keeps them in kennels, so they had never seen a movie and they loved it. They absolutely *loved* it.'

'Can I come to your house to watch a movie?' Lulu asked coyly.

Jimmy was doubtful. He'd had other dogs in, especially Paddy. Being Irish, Paddy liked to watch the Gold Cup at Cheltenham. But he had never had a bitch in.

'I suppose you could both come,' he said doubtfully.

'We don't want her,' Lulu said. 'She'll have us watching ballet and documentaries and stuff like that.'

‘Well,’ Jimmy said, ‘if she likes ballet...’

‘If she comes to my house,’ Lulu said scornfully, ‘she’ll watch Hannah Montana like everyone else.’

‘Can we stop this nonsense?’ Ria said. ‘This rescue act sounds very exciting and we want to be part of it. We want jobs to do.’

‘Yes,’ Lulu said, ‘and if your boss doesn’t find us something we’ll just turn up and get in the way.’

Jimmy was worried now. ‘As I said, we’re hoping to free the six pups. Perhaps once they’re out you two can take care of them.’

‘What!’ Lulu exploded in disgust.

‘Jimmy,’ Ria said quietly, ‘you don’t realise how insulting, how patronising that is.’

‘But that’s what bitches do,’ Jimmy said defensively. ‘They take care of the little ones.’

‘In the past maybe,’ Lulu said. ‘Not any more.’

‘Have you never heard of feminism?’ Ria asked. ‘We’re going to form our own group. We’re going to call it “Girl Power”.’

‘Yeah, here come the girls!’ Lulu exclaimed.

It was a bright April morning when it all began. There was a hint of showers in the air but the daffodils were in full bloom and Jimmy was delighted to chase an early butterfly, though he knew he could never catch it.

At the copse before anyone else, he was a little worried that things might not work out as planned. Everyone knew what they had to do and there was no reason why things should go wrong. But as Chalkie would say, quoting that Scottish poet he was so fond of, *The best laid plans of mice and men gang aft agley*, which roughly translated means, no matter how well you plan ahead things can go wrong.

Don Schnauzer and The Professor seemed more confident, but they hadn't met Rocky and Rambo. Fortunately Max, the German shepherd had. He had been to the wire fence with Jimmy and they had got along fine.

Max was a big dog and his presence had commanded respect. The two Rottweilers listened enraptured to his tales of exciting exploits in the Army and in the police force.

You don't want to be with Charlie Spence, he told them. You should first join the Army. You would have your own handler who would take good care of you. He would teach you all you need to know. You would learn how to sniff out bombs and things. It's great fun and handlers absolutely love their dogs.

Or you could be a police dog. Police dog handlers are the same. A handler and his dog are great mates and in the police force you can have lots of fun catching scallys. Then when you get too old for all that, he told them, you can do what I did. You can become a guide dog. It's a pretty responsible job but it's not a bad life.

Rocky and Rambo had listened intently as a whole new future of brighter prospects seemed to open up for them and Jimmy was grateful. He felt more sure of them now.

'Ah, they are all right,' Max told him. 'They are not stupid. They are just innocent, that's all. They will be there when we need them. I am sure of that.'

Paddy, with the help of Rhavi and Ringo, had done his job and the supermarket trolley was in position behind a large bush near the gates to Spence's place.

Dogs from all around had been invited to join in an operation to rescue some very young dogs from ill treatment at the hands of a brutish owner, and the response had been overwhelming. Many breeds of all shapes and sizes were now converging on Warkwood and Ringo and Rhavi were directing them to where they could lie in wait along the lane.

Ria and Lulu had badgered Don Schnauzer and The Professor until they got their way. They had been given jobs lecturing the newcomers on the evils of dogfighting and then, when everything was set, they took up their vantage points as 'look-outs', Lulu halfway down the lane, Ria nearer the village. Their job was to alert the others if Charlie Spence returned unexpectedly.

By three o'clock that afternoon everything was ready. Everyone obeyed orders, stayed out of sight and remained as quiet as they possibly could. In command, Don Schnauzer and The Professor sat out of sight in long grass on the higher bank of the lane, waiting for Spence's van to appear and set off for the village.

Their biggest stroke of luck had come earlier that morning when Max and Jimmy spoke to the two Rottweilers and learned that the wooden gates were operated by a dibber. Rocky and Rambo had no idea what a dibber was until Jimmy explained it was like the thing they saw him use to operate the television.

'Spence uses one of those,' Rambo told them.

Apparently there was a key pad on the inside of the gate. Max drew an oblong in the soil and, guessing there would be ten, he marked the buttons out in a 3-3-3-1 formation.

'Is it like this?' he asked.

'No,' Rambo said confidently. 'Two on the bottom row.'

Max nodded and made it 3-3-3-2. The extra one was probably there to cancel and start again. 'And which one does he hit?'

'Oh, I don't know,' Rambo said. 'He does something like this.' He pointed a paw. Top left, top right, middle left, middle right.

'Just four?'

Rambo nodded 'Yeah, definite.'

'I've never seen him do that,' Rocky said.

'Maybe you're not as observant as I am,' Rambo said, his nose in the air, suddenly superior and pleased to be taken seriously.

Max looked at Jimmy. 'We can try it. It would be much simpler if we could get the trolley inside the place instead of having to bring the pups out one by one.'

It was soon after three o'clock when the gate opened and Spence's van emerged. Everyone was alert but lying low, out of sight, as the gate closed behind him and he drove off towards the village. The problem was they had no idea what time he would be back. Before he was banned from the Black Bull it was fine. They knew it would be late, seven o'clock at least. But now, once he had been to the village store, he had nowhere else to go.

Ria watched him leave the lane and turn towards the village before she signalled 'All clear' to Lulu. Lulu then passed the message on to Ringo and at once all the recruited dogs popped up from the longish grass like dozens of meerkats, wondering what would happen next.

As soon as they got the all clear, Rocky and Rambo began the task of scooping out more earth from the hole under the wire to make the entrance bigger. Jimmy crawled under the wire to join them but before helping them out he trotted over to the gate. On his hind legs he tried different combinations on the key pad, starting with the top left, but without success.

It was then that things started to go wrong. The dogs recruited as volunteer helpers were restless, not willing to wait and flood the lane only if Spence's van appeared. In a mass of flailing legs, madly wagging tails and excited barking, they came out from the grassy banks and descended on the lane like troops going 'over the top' on a battlefield.

And just at that moment Jimmy, still prodding frantically at the key pad, was surprised to hit the correct combination and see the wooden gate slowly opened inwards.

Hordes of dogs of all shapes and sizes squeezed through the widening gap in a great crush to flood the smallholding, and some of those who had their orders and knew what they were supposed to do next were unable to get through.

Jimmy was clinging to the back of the gate. He had been as surprised as anyone when the gate suddenly opened and now he was anxiously trying to recall what numbers he had hit. He knew he had hit one, three and four in that order but he had slipped as he hit the last one and he was not sure what it was.

It was turning into a riot of a party with dogs barking and chasing each other all over Charlie Spence's property. Jimmy saw what was happening and he signalled frantically to Rocky and Rambo and fought his way through to get to them.

'This is crazy,' he called, out of breath. 'You're going to have to scare them out of our way'

'No problem,' Rocky called back and he started to growl and bare his teeth at the revellers around him as Rambo joined in.

Most of the dogs backed off but one snappy little terrier was spoiling for a fight. Rocky and Rambo raised their eyes skywards in exasperation. With a joint sigh they each took one end of the little agitator and cast him, wriggling and squealing, aside.

A path was beginning to emerge ahead of them now as they made their way to the sheds. Jimmy said he would try to bring the trolley in and he struggled back towards the gate.

'Paddy!' he cried as he spotted Paddy looking bewildered out in the lane. 'Paddy! Bring the trolley!'

Paddy signalled he had understood and with Rhavi he retrieved the trolley from its hiding place and unceremoniously they pushed it ahead of them into the crowd calling, 'Ambulance Service! Make way, please!' And surprisingly many of the out of control dogs did, stepping out of the way and taking others with them.

Jimmy directed them towards the sheds and soon they had the trolley in place and ready. Rocky and Rambo gently gripped a pup each by the neck, carried them to the door and placed them in the trolley. It wasn't easy because the pups were so young they had barely any fur, but the Rottweilers were extremely gentle with them and soon all six were huddled close together, unharmed and unaware of what was going on.

Paddy and Rhavi took over now, turning the trolley and pushing ahead into the confusion of the crowd. Barking angry commands at anyone who impeded their progress they forced a way towards the exit.

The Rottweilers were already at the next shed, trying to release the two older pit bulls as Jimmy closed the door on the prying eyes of the curious. Rocky and Rambo tried hard to opcn up the cages but they were getting nowhere.

Then Jimmy noticed the cages were bottomless and it occurred to him to turn them over.

Under Jimmy's direction all three gripped the side of the first cage and tried to lift it, but it was too heavy. At first they found they could raise it only slightly. But they refused to be beaten and with one concerted effort they succeeded in raising the cage another couple of inches and somehow the young pit bull managed to get his head under and struggle out.

'Me! Me!' the other one cried. 'What about me?'

'All right, all right,' Rocky told him. 'We're coming.'

Again they raised the cage just a few inches and the second pit bull struggled through. Out of habit the freed pit bulls faced each other as if ready to fight, but Jimmy stepped between them.

'Listen, you two,' he warned them, 'just remember that you are friends now and friends look out for each other. We are going to take you to the village vet and he will take good care of you. So you behave yourselves and do as you're told. Okay?'

They both nodded meekly as Rocky and Rambo stood over them.

'Run off,' Rocky said, 'and the police or the warden will get you.'

'Yeah,' Rambo said, 'and they might think you're dangerous dogs and have you put down.'

'So you stay with us now,' Jimmy warned them, 'and, as I said, you do exactly as you're told. Okay?'

Again they nodded in agreement.

So far so good, thought Jimmy. Perhaps it would be a good idea to get all these party mad dogs to leave now. Mission accomplished. But it was not over yet.

At the village end of the lane Ria was barking frantically and as loud as her small ladylike voice would allow. She was desperately trying to alert everyone to the fact that Charlie Spence's van had just entered the lane and he was heading home.

Spence pulled up sharply as his way was blocked by a great crowd of dogs. He sounded his horn angrily, wondering what was going on. He tried to inch his van forward but most of the recruited dogs who were still in the lane remembered why they were there.

They closed up in a solid block of bodies, making it impossible for him to move forward without mowing them down. Spence was furious, sorely tempted to do just that, but even he knew he dare not. He climbed out of his seat and tried to see what was happening ahead, but all he could see all along the lane was dogs, dogs and more dogs.

He left his cab and clambered up the grassy bank, leather belt in hand, lashing out at any dog that got in his way. The dogs grouped together, forcing him upwards to the higher ground and it was from here he could see that fifty yards away the entrance to his property was wide open and the place was overflowing with dogs.

Shouting and swearing in fury he lashed out again and again and was forced higher up the bank. Then as he ran, fell, picked himself up and scrambled over dog after dog he couldn't believe his eyes. A supermarket trolley was being pushed out of his gate by two dogs on their hind legs and other dogs were clearing the way.

Puzzled at first he saw, as he fought to get closer, that six small bundles were huddled in a corner of the shallow tray. They were *his* puppies, *his* little fight prospects and they were being stolen. At this he went completely berserk and he ran, stumbling and falling and picking himself up and falling again, until lashing out at anything and everything in his way he reached the open gate.

Along with Jimmy the young pit bulls were just emerging. They saw Spence and exchanged looks. 'Let's get him!' one said.

But Jimmy cried, 'No!' and bringing up the rear, Rocky and Rambo steered them away and towards the hole under the fence which by now, with the gate congested, was the best way out.

Charlie Spence came running forward, still astounded, unable to understand what was happening. All he knew was that he was being robbed. He ran to the empty sheds to confirm what he knew already. The puppies had gone. The two partly trained pit bulls, he found, were also missing, their cages empty.

There was a fight in Scotland in a month's time and he had planned to have one ready to take part. One was emerging as the better fighter of the two, able to inflict the most damage on the other and getting fiercer all the time. He had high hopes of that one and he had already paid a hundred pounds to enter him in the Scottish contest. He wanted him there to win back at least the entrance fee and maybe land the big prize.

He ran back around the sheds to where dozens of dogs were still milling about, trespassing and trampling over his property, when across the compound he caught sight of his guard dogs, Rocky and Rambo. What were these two useless idiots doing? he asked himself. They should never have let this happen.

Calling them by name he ran towards them, arms waving, and the two Rottweilers stopped in their tracks. Slowly they turned and stared back at him with looks of utter contempt.

'You were supposed to take care of this place,' he roared. 'Now clear this lot out. Do you hear? Do your job!'

But they bared their teeth, growled low and put on the most fearsome looks they could muster. Then they moved slightly towards him as if they were about to tear him apart.

Spence opened his mouth to speak but he was scared now and he turned and ran towards the bungalow. Seconds later he emerged with an air rifle and began firing wildly into the crowd. The dogs scattered, running for the exit, barking and howling, desperate to escape.

Jimmy was at the wire fence as the pit bulls and the Rottweilers followed each other through.

'He's got a gun,' Rocky told him.

'Maybe we should go back and get him,' Rambo said. 'Sort him out once and for all.'

'No,' Jimmy said. 'You can't. You know that. Harm a human and you're in trouble.'

'A *human*?' Rocky said scornfully.

'Yes,' Jimmy said with a wry smile, 'even someone like Spence.'

He nodded encouragingly at the young pit bulls. 'Well done, you two.' To Rocky and Rambo he said, 'The gang are gathering on the road. Report to Don Schnauzer or The Professor and you can all go down to the village vet together.'

'*All* of us?' Rocky asked.

'No, no,' Jimmy said. 'Ringo is asking all the volunteers to go home. Their work is done.'

'What about you?' Rambo asked.

'I'm coming, too. I just want to make sure everyone is out of here. I think most of the gang are safe and you four are okay, although no one has seen Chalkie. He's probably all right.' He smiled. 'He's so small you sometimes can't see him in all that long grass. Anyway you go and I'll catch up with you later.'

He went back under the fence and peered out from behind a bush. The crowd of dogs had thinned dramatically. Just a few stragglers remained, dodging round Spence and running for the exit, some of them howling as they were hit by stinging pellets.

But then Spence ran out of pellets and he fumbled furiously with his hand-held key pad. His head swirling in a murderous rage, he prodded out the combination of numbers and slowly the big gate began to close. The remaining dogs raced madly to the narrowing exit and Jimmy was pleased and satisfied to see that they all got through before the big gate finally swung into place.

He breathed a sigh of relief and he was about to turn back to the hole under the fence when he was transfixed, horrified by what he saw. Running as fast as his little legs could carry him was Chalkie. But the exit was closed and the little Scottie was trapped and at the mercy of the evil Spence.

An expression of glee had spread over Spence's crazed face and there was no doubt he was about to vent his full fury on the little Scot. Chalkie cowered back, looking even smaller against

the wide gate as Spence advanced, clearly enjoying his intended victim's terror. Chalkie was trapped. There was nowhere to run to and with a vicious glint in his eye and having lost all control, this madman was wielding a leather strap with thick metal studs.

There were no other dogs to come to Chalkie's aid. There was only Jimmy. But Jimmy was quick to react. He sprinted from his hiding place and just as Spence raised his arm, holding high his deadly strap and about to strike the Scottie down, Jimmy leapt through the air and sank his teeth into Spence's tattooed flesh.

Spence squealed in pain as he fought to shake Jimmy off but Jimmy sank his teeth still deeper and the blood spurted down Spence's arm. Then, as Spence dropped to his knees, Jimmy let go and ran to Chalkie who was shaking visibly, his mouth open in horror, as Jimmy hurried him from the scene.

Writhing on the floor, holding his injured arm as if mortally wounded, Charlie Spence was whimpering like a baby. 'I know you!' he screamed at Jimmy. 'And I'll have you! You're dead!' he cried and a stream of dreadful abuse followed.

Jimmy directed Chalkie to the hole under the wire, Chalkie apologising profusely. 'Ach, I'm sorry, Jimmy. I shouldn'y have been there. I should have got out much sooner. And now I've got you in terrible trouble. It's all my fault.'

'He deserved it,' Jimmy said, though he hated the thought of having sunk his teeth into Spence and he wanted to rush to the nearest stream and wash his mouth out.

'I am so so sorry,' Chalkie was saying, genuinely remorseful. 'I should never have been there.'

'It's all right,' Jimmy said, though he knew it wasn't. He had attacked a man and he knew the consequences. From now on he was a marked dog.

CHAPTER NINE

Don Schnauzer was quite old now and he had paid several visits to the village vet in recent years. He knew the vet, Mr Hill, and Mr Hill knew him. The outer door to the surgery was open. With the two young pit bulls in tow he tapped his paw on the glass inner door and with a bright smile Mr Hill's receptionist, Mary, let him in. From behind him Don Schnauzer ushered in the two pit bulls.

Mr Hill appeared at the door to his inner sanctum. 'Well, hello there!' he said. 'What have we here?'

There were few appointments that afternoon and the surgery had been quiet. But it wouldn't be for much longer. Mr Hill came from behind his counter and bent down to pat The Don and cast an eye over the others. Then he went to the door to look for the owner of the pit bulls, or perhaps Don Schnauzer's owner, but there was no one there.

'What have you brought me, Don?' he asked and he saw at once the badly torn ear and the deep open wound that had been so slow to heal. He went down on one knee and his practised eye saw other wounds and bruises and he knew he was looking at two severely maltreated dogs.

He went to the door again and looked out but there was still no sign of any owner. There were a couple of local dogs he knew well, a bloodhound and a beagle, but that was all. He went back inside and looked knowingly at Don Schnauzer, convinced The Don was trying to tell him something. If only he could talk, he thought with a smile.

'Come on,' he said to all three. 'Let's find you a drink and something to eat.'

Mr Hill and Mary watched as the two pit bulls ate ravenously and Mr Hill realised that these dogs were being trained to take part in dogfights.

'Mary,' he said quietly, 'I believe these dogs are being groomed to take part in illegal dogfights and, as far as we know, we have only one suspect in that department.'

'Charlie Spence,' Mary said.

Mr Hill nodded solemnly. 'Will you get me Sergeant Evans on the telephone, please? I think we might at last have some solid evidence regarding our Mr Spence and his evil pursuits.'

Max the German shepherd took the Rottweilers to Bramble. He knew the police dogs based at the main station there and he was hoping they would help place his two protégées.

'Not so fast, you two,' he complained. 'I'm not used to walking this far these days.'

Rocky and Rambo slowed down. They were enjoying their new freedom and they were interested in everything that was going on around them. They soon noticed though that people tended to shy away and some even crossed the road at their approach. They were hurt and saddened by this reaction and they wanted to put things right. 'Not exactly pleased to see us, are they?' Rocky said.

'No,' Rambo moaned. 'And it's not very nice, is it?'

'I know how you feel,' Max said. 'Some people are scared of German shepherds. Mind you, some people are scared of their own shadows.'

'But they don't like us, do they?' Rocky insisted.

'No, they don't, and that's because you have this awful reputation. For Rottweilers everywhere, it's up to you to prove them wrong. No matter what, you must remember that you are nice dogs and you like people. You don't want to scare them and they have absolutely no reason to be afraid of you.'

'Yeah,' Rambo said, 'if they'll ever believe us.'

They were approaching a primary school and it was home time.

The playground was full of small children rushing out to be met and embraced by doting parents. Now, as they saw the daunting trio – two Rottweilers and a German shepherd – the parents and teachers huddled the children together and one teacher rushed forward to close the school gates. Some parents, seeing their children were safe, stayed in their cars.

Max put his head down with his nose to the railing and several small children rushed forward to stroke him as their helpless and worried parents looked on. Rocky and Rambo put their heads down, too, as little hands reached out to stroke them.

Then a man who hadn't registered what was happening drove up, jumped from his car and was a little surprised to be greeted fondly by Max. He stroked Max for a moment and only then did he sense the tension behind the rail. When first Rocky and then Rambo put their heads down he had no option but to stroke them, too.

'Okay,' Max whispered after a moment. 'That's enough. Let's go.'

The Rottweilers followed, their tails wagging as lots of children called out and waved them goodbye.

'It's called Public Relations,' Max told them as they went on their way. 'It's all about image, the way people see you. You have to win people over. It's not easy, but you two seem pretty good at it.'

At the police headquarters Max was greeted by a number of old friends, both handlers and dogs. To one large dog he called, 'Hey, Butch! Over here.'

The big dog ambled over. 'Max! How are you doing, old timer?'

'I've brought you a couple of new recruits,' Max said. 'They want to be police dogs, join the force.'

Butch looked them over. 'They're a big weedy,' he said. 'They could do with building up a bit.'

'I don't think their owner fed them very well,' Max told him.

'They'll be all right here,' Butch said. 'But they'll have to learn to do as they're told.'

'They can do that,' Max assured him and the Rottweilers nodded their heads.

There were two handlers at the base and they came out now to see what was going on.

'Hey!' one said in surprise. 'Where did you two come from?'

Rocky put his head down and the handler patted him fondly and knelt to give him a hug. Rambo pestered the other handler until he laughed and did the same.

The handlers felt the Rottweilers' collars and read from their metal discs. 'This one's called Rocky and he belongs to Charlie Spence,' one said.

'So does this one,' said the other, 'and he's called Rambo.'

'We'd better get them some grub,' the first one said. 'What do you reckon they're doing up here?'

'I don't know,' the other said, 'but there was something going on over in Warkwood. Serge says he had a report that hundreds of dogs were roaming around the village. Seems they were not causing any trouble or anything. They were just there and no one seems to know why.'

The sergeant appeared now and told one of them he had a job for him. 'Couple of CID lads are going to Warkwood and they reckon you might be needed.'

The handler explained that Rocky and Rambo had turned up 'out of the blue' and they belonged to Charlie Spence.

The sergeant nodded knowingly. 'In that case we'll keep them here for now. Make sure they get a drink and something to eat.'

The handler who brought his van round and opened the rear

door for his dog to jump in looked at Max. 'Do you want a lift home, Max?' he asked.

Max was more than grateful. He was not looking forward to the long walk back to Warkwood. He smiled brightly, his tail wagging as he bade goodbye and the best of luck to Rocky and to Rambo before jumping aboard the van and settling back, satisfied with a job well done.

Charlie Spence had arrived at the medical centre in the village demanding to see a doctor. Though the surgery was full and he refused to wait his turn, he created such a fuss that the practice nurse, probably to get rid of him, agreed to dress his wound and give him a tetanus injection.

'Probably the dog that needs an injection,' she muttered to a colleague before silently performing her duty.

Spence was telling anyone who would listen that he had been savaged by a mad dog. Some kind of collie it was, he said, and it was a local dog. He'd seen it around the village.

When he arrived at the police station he was still in a furious rage. His property had been broken into and badly damaged. His precious puppies had been stolen and he had been attacked by a crazed animal. What were they going to do about it? he demanded to know. He wanted action and he wanted it NOW!

The constable on the desk patiently took down his statement and assured him he would be informed of any developments.

'Any developments!' he raged. 'I want that dog found and put down. It's a dangerous beast and it must be destroyed.'

The constable listened without comment then said, 'We understand your puppies are with Mr Hill.'

'Right!' he said and at that he stormed out shouting, 'Put down! *Destroyed*! I want that dog destroyed! Do y'hear?'

People in the vicinity couldn't fail to hear and many in the village had come to their doors aware that something was happening but not sure what. The rumour was that a mad dog was on the loose. Already it had savagely attacked a local man, almost ripping off his arm. But the surge of sympathy subsided somewhat when it became known that the man in question was Charlie Spence.

Outside the village vet's surgery, Spence pulled up in his battered van and blustered his way inside demanding, 'Where are my puppies?'

Mary was frightened of him and didn't know what to say but Mr Hill appeared and faced him unperturbed. 'The puppies are here, Mr Spence,' he said calmly, 'and they are quite safe.'

'Right! So bring 'em out. I want them and I want them *now*!'

'I have your six puppies, Mr Spence.' Mr Hill produced two large photographs of the two pit bulls and their wounds. 'I also have your young pit bulls. And at this moment they are being treated for serious injuries.'

An athletic-looking young man who was working in the surgery on a week's work experience appeared at the inner door. 'Is that him?' he asked aggressively. 'Is he the owner?'

'It's all right, Edward,' Mr Hill said. 'Go back to your work.'

There was a moment's silence as Mary the receptionist and dedicated animal lover, Mr Hill the highly regarded veterinary surgeon, and Edward the angry young man looked at Spence as if awaiting an explanation. Spence was prepared to bluster his way through this, but there was something else. Something was making him feel distinctly uneasy and he was not sure what it was.

Don Schnauzer was sitting quietly in a corner of the small reception area. He was looking up at Spence, his eyes boring into the back of Spence's shaven head. Spence looked round quickly and was startled by the look in Don Schnauzer's eyes.

There was something scary and unnerving about it, as if the dog knew all his secrets and was bent on retribution.

'What are you looking at?' Spence asked dismissively, but Don Schnauzer's eyes didn't waver.

'Perhaps he knows what you've been up to,' Mr Hill said.

'I've had enough of this,' Spence declared. His anger was back and mounting, but he was less sure of himself now, not wanting to challenge Mr Hill's implied accusation. 'Those dogs are my property and I want them *now*. Or else.'

Mr Hill smiled tolerantly. 'Or else what, Mr Spence?'

But before Spence could reply the outer door opened and the two CID officers from Bramble walked in.

'Good morning, Mr Hill,' the older of the two said.

'Morning, officer,' Mr Hill said brightly and Mary relaxed.

The detective looked at Charlie Spence. 'Ah, Mr Spence. We have met before, have we not?'

'I've nothing to say to you,' Spence said belligerently.

'But we have something to say to you,' the detective said and he turned to his colleague.

The younger officer stepped forward. 'Charles Albert Spence, I am arresting you on suspicion of organising and taking part in illegal dogfighting. You are also arrested on suspicion of illegally training dogs in your care for this purpose, and on suspicion of causing unnecessary suffering to animals in your care and...'

Don Schnauzer's eyes were shining behind their thin veil of hair and his tail was wagging as it hadn't wagged in a long time. With a huge smile he looked across at Mr Hill and, as if he knew and understood everything that had happened, as if they shared equally in the satisfaction of seeing a man like Spence arrested, Mr Hill nodded and smiled back.

CHAPTER TEN

Don Schnauzer was happy with the outcome of the operation but he was saddened, too. It had not been achieved without cost. Jimmy was the loser and it was so unfair. Jimmy was such a fine, honest, upstanding and totally reliable young dog. He was not dangerous in any way. He had simply gone to the aid of a friend and for that he was condemned, condemned to be hunted down like a common criminal. A way must be found to shield him from the consequences of his bravery and help him escape.

Chalkie was inconsolable. He blamed himself for what happened. He blamed himself for being in the wrong place at the wrong time and he blamed himself for being so slow to get out. Jimmy was in terrible trouble because of him and there was little or nothing he could do about it. The others had tried to console him but nothing helped and he was the saddest little dog in the whole of the country.

The hunt was on with a vengeance now. People in the village and beyond were suddenly wary of taking walks by the river or in the lovely countryside, alone or with their dogs. Already there were lurid tales and alleged sightings of a wild dog with fangs dripping blood roaming free as far as Bramble and the city.

People were warned, too, on television and on local radio to take extra care, to be sure doors were securely locked night and day and not to leave their windows open. Farmers and keepers of livestock took out their guns ready for any unwelcome intruder. And a picture of a dog that was not quite a collie and looked remarkably like Jimmy appeared in the local newspaper and on posters displayed at various vantage points around the village.

'Dogfather,' Chalkie asked sadly, 'do you think they will know it was Jimmy?'

'If Spence gives a description, Mr Hill will know right away.'

'Mr Hill is a good man,' Chalkie said. 'He knows what Spence is like. Maybe he'll no identify Jimmy to the police.'

'He has to,' The Don said. 'It's his job.'

'Perhaps we will have to hide Jimmy for a while,' The Professor said, 'until all this blows over.'

Don Schnauzer shook his head. 'I don't think so. Jimmy is going to have to go away, but to where I don't know.'

Jimmy was at home, sitting quietly in front of the television with his owners. But he was not watching the programme. He was confused. His head was full of conflicting ideas and unworkable plans. He didn't know what to do. He didn't know what was going to happen and he knew in his heart that he couldn't stay. He was already a fugitive and he would have to go. But to where? One thing was certain: this easy way of life was coming to an end.

The door bell rang. Jimmy looked at his owners. Arthur looked at Doreen and Doreen looked at him. They didn't usually have visitors this time of night. Slowly Arthur dragged himself from his easy chair and moved the living room curtain aside to look through the window. Eyebrows raised, he glanced back at Doreen then went to the door.

Jimmy heard voices. 'Dangerous dog' were two of the words that stood out and he guessed it was the police. He stood up casually, stretched himself and ambled into the kitchen.

'Yeah, sure,' he heard Arthur say. 'He's around somewhere.'

Jimmy didn't wait. He went through to the outhouse, up on to the tumble dryer, through the window, his escape hatch, and out into the very dark night.

Down the side of the house he could see part of a police van. He turned and ran the length of the garden and through the hole in the hedge. He shivered in the chill night air. Where to go? That was the question. He wanted somewhere warm and dry, somewhere where he could sit down and think, decide what he was going to do.

It had been raining and the pavements shone wet in the moonlight. He thought of Rhavi's cellar. He was sure Rhavi would let him spend the night there but the village store was closed and in darkness and there was no sign of Rhavi.

From the light of a street lamp he saw a poster in the window of a shop nearby. HAVE YOU SEEN THIS DOG? it read and there was a picture of a Border collie. Jimmy stood quite still, looking at it critically for a moment. It wasn't really like him, he decided, but it was near enough to make people look at him and wonder. When he was in the garden earlier in the day the lady next door was looking at him curiously and now he knew why.

He shivered and he realised it was quite cold. He knew he had to get away but he needed time to think, to plan his escape, and for now the only place he could think of was the copse, the gang headquarters. It was still cold but at least it was not raining as he settled down for the night. The thick bushes and the overhanging branches of a cluster of trees made the copse private in a way, but it was not what he had at home. He lay there, quite still, all alone in the dark, listening to the noises of the night and wondering what the new day would bring.

He kept drifting off and waking with a start, but he must have finally fallen asleep because when he opened his eyes he could see through the branches of the trees above that the sky was much brighter and it must be morning. He stretched a little, sat up and came face to face with a rabbit. The rabbit looked startled, caught and held as if hypnotised by his gaze. Then it turned and fled.

Jimmy laughed. The poor thing looked as though he knew he was staring into the face of madness, a ferocious killer dog. But then he thought, more soberly, he was a rogue dog, a dog on the run, a hunted animal, wanted by the police. Yet he didn't feel any different than he did before he bit Spence and he certainly didn't feel any remorse. If he had to do it again to save Chalkie or any of his friends he knew he would.

Around mid-morning there was a rustling sound from nearby. Jimmy sat up, alerted. It was Ringo the Beagle and he greeted Jimmy warmly and with affection. 'The whole gang is meeting here at eleven,' he said. 'We have to decide what we are going to do with you.'

'Oh, do you?' Jimmy said with a smile. 'Don't I have a say?'

'Well,' Ringo said, 'you know what I mean. The boss says we have to help you get away from around here.'

The clock on the church tower in the village began to strike eleven and as the last stroke died away Ringo went a little way out of the copse and did his distinctive clarion call, his three barks repeated ten seconds later.

Rhavi was the first to arrive. 'Jimmy!' he cried. 'Great to see you are okay. Have you eaten yet?'

Jimmy shook his head and Rhavi dashed off at once. The Dogfather himself and The Professor were next to arrive and they, too, were delighted to see him. Then Chalkie came in and at once ran to him, lowering his head.

'Ach, Jimmy,' he said. 'What can I say? I could kill myself.'

'No way,' Jimmy said in alarm. 'We just did what we had to do. You mustn't blame yourself for anything.'

'But I do,' Chalkie said, his tears flowing. 'It's all my fault.'

'What is done is done,' Don Schnauzer said. 'Now let us get down to business.'

Max reported first. 'The Rottweilers are in good hands,' he announced. 'I took them to the police headquarters in Bramble.

The police know they belonged to Charlie Spence and they won't be sending them back. I'm pretty sure they will be given jobs with their own handlers. It may not be in Bramble or around here. It could be anywhere. But they'll be fine.'

'Good,' Don Schnauzer said. 'Well done, Max. Now I was at Mr Hill's place when Spence was arrested. Mr Hill, I'm sure, will find good homes for the six puppies. And Spence won't be getting the older pit bulls back either. They will stay with Mr Hill until their wounds have healed. Then they, too, will be found good homes.'

The dogs were nodding their heads and barking in approval as Rhavi came running in with a big bag of dog food. 'This is from the shop. Ali won't miss it.'

'Oh great!' Ringo said, stepping forward.

'It's not for you, you fool,' Rhavi told him. 'It's for Jimmy. He hasn't had anything to eat.'

There was the usual whirlwind arrival now and Paddy came tumbling in. 'Sorry I'm late, boss,' he gasped. 'But I've got a great idea, so I have.'

'What's that thing around your neck?' Rhavi asked.

Paddy was wearing a black and white striped football scarf. 'Ah, well, 'tis all part of the plan, so 'tis.' To Don Shnauzer he said, 'Dogfather, you remember last night we were discussing putting Jimmy on a goods train south? Well, how about this for an idea? Today is Saturday, right? And there's a big football match this afternoon. Well, there'll be a train full of football fans going to the match. They'll all be wearing their black and white striped scarves, so they will. You know what they're like. So I suggest Jimmy wears this scarf and just climbs aboard the train. No need to smuggle him aboard.'

Ringo had the football scarf around his neck. 'Hey, it's good this. Where did you get it?'

‘Don’t ask,’ Paddy said, taking it back.

‘I’m no sure dogs are allowed on trains,’ Chalkie said quietly.

‘Listen,’ Rhavi said, ‘if he’s wearing a black and white scarf I don’t reckon anyone would dare order him off a *football* train. Not around here anyway. You know what they’re like. Football crazy, all of ’em.’

‘Exactly,’ Paddy agreed.

‘I think this is a very good idea, Paddy,’ The Professor said.

‘Yes,’ Don Schnauzer. ‘If Jimmy was on a goods train he might be spotted. But if he’s on a passenger train full of football fans he won’t be hiding and he’ll get to the city that way.’

‘And another thing,’ Max said soberly, ‘it is much easier to survive living rough in the city than out in the country. There are more places to sleep at night where it is warmer and drier. Shop doorways and warehouses and derelict buildings. There are more cafes and restaurants where you can pick up scraps of food, too.’

‘Sounds like the voice of experience,’ Rhavi said with a smile.

‘I have seen this, Rhavi,’ Max said. ‘When I was with the police force we would sometimes search these places for criminals in hiding or people dealing in drugs, that sort of thing. I have seen dogs living like this. They would tell me they had no place to go and we would leave them alone. We were not looking for dogs.’

So that was decided. Jimmy would wear Paddy’s scarf and he would catch the two o’clock football special from the local station.

‘One thing though.’ Rhavi stepped forward and raised a paw to Jimmy’s collar. ‘We need to get rid of this. If we take this off he can’t be identified.’

‘And how do we do that?’ Ringo asked.

‘Leave it to me,’ Rhavi said and with his magician’s touch he swiftly removed Jimmy’s collar.

'So what do you think, Jimmy?' Don Schnauzer asked. 'Are you happy with all this?'

'I suppose it's the best I can hope for,' Jimmy said. 'There'll be other strays in the city, I expect. I should be able to make a few friends, learn a few tricks.' He hesitated. 'There is something though, Dogfather.'

The Don's veiled eyes softened. 'What is it, son?'

'I would... er... I would really like to see Ria. You know, the King Charles. Just once, before I leave.'

The Professor was shaking his head.

'It would be very dangerous,' The Don said to discourage him.

'It's impossible,' Rhavi said. 'It's not safe out there.'

'Bitches,' Ringo said scornfully. 'They always get in the way.'

'I could arrange it, so I could,' Paddy said after a moment. 'I could go with him, keep a look-out.'

'I would really like to see her,' Jimmy said.

'Then it's up to you, son,' The Don said. 'It's your decision. But if you do decide to see her you must be very, very careful.'

'We'd better get going then' Paddy said. 'The train's at two.'

The members of the gang stepped forward, one by one, to place a paw on Jimmy's left shoulder in a dog-style *hug* and wish him luck.

Chalkie couldn't reach but Jimmy crouched down, whispered in his ear, 'Goodbye, Chalkie. We'll always be friends.'

Chalkie could only nod in response, his eyes filled with tears.

Don Schnauzer came last. He put a paw on Jimmy's shoulder. 'Good luck, son,' he said. 'Wherever you go may good fortune go with you. We will never forget you.'

Lulu was stretched out luxuriously on her woolly rug. Her mistress, a frothy blonde girl with her fingernails and toenails painted black, was on the telephone, prattling away as usual to one of her girlfriends. She was a bit silly, empty headed, thought Lulu. But she was nice and she loved Lulu and Lulu loved her.

The trouble was, she was always prancing about the village with Lulu trailing behind on a fancy lead. Lulu was expected to do her silly walk with her head in the air. Her mistress walked a bit like that herself, Lulu often thought. All she needed was a pompom stuck on her bottom.

There were two short barks that Lulu recognised at once. She went to the window, her front paws on the ledge. Paddy was in the road outside.

'It's your boyfriend,' her mistress said, opening the side door. 'We're going out soon remember.'

The mistress went back in the house, saying into the telephone, 'It's Lulu. Her boyfriend's here. Honestly, I don't know what she sees in him. A big daft Irish setter. Anyway, I was telling you…'

'Hi, Paddy!' Lulu said. 'What's up?'

'I've got Jimmy,' he said.

'Where? Where is he? Is he all right?'

'Yeah, he's okay, so he is. But listen, he has to leave the village and he's going now, this afternoon. He wants to see Ria before he goes.'

'Wait here,' Lulu said.

Ria had been desperately worried, inconsolable, since all this began. If she hadn't asked Jimmy for help in the first place, she had wailed to Lulu, he wouldn't be in this terrible trouble now.

Lulu scurried down the side of the house and into the bushes that divided her house and garden from Ria's. She barked softly, but there was no response. Lulu was frantic. She knew how Ria felt about Jimmy. She knew that Jimmy had to go; there was no way he could stay after what happened with Spence. But she knew, too, that Ria would be devastated if she didn't see him before he left.

Ria had heard Lulu's call and she was scratching noisily at the back door in an effort to attract attention. Her mistress was out but Robert, her master, was asleep in the armchair in the living room, a newspaper covering his face. She looked around for a way to wake him and saw his golf bag. Move that and you're in trouble, her mistress often said. So she pushed it over and it clattered to the floor, his precious golf balls spilling out and rolling across the tiles.

Robert awoke with a start and came into the kitchen as Ria began to scratch again at the door. 'Hello,' he said sleepily. 'What's going on here then? You want to go out, sweetheart?'

He opened the door to the rear garden and Ria dashed out.

Lulu was waiting anxiously in the bushes. 'Jimmy's here,' she said quietly. 'He's going away today. Right now in fact. But he wants to see you before he goes.'

Ria's eyes filled up. 'Is he all right?'

'I don't know,' Lulu said. 'He's with Paddy. You wait here.'

She went to the front of the house where Paddy was waiting. 'Bring him over,' she said quietly, 'and be careful.'

Jimmy was watching from the wooded stretch that led down to the river on the other side of the road. He looked left and right. There was no one about. Then, at Paddy's signal, he raced across the road and jumped over the garden wall to follow Lulu down the side of the house and into the bushes where he came face to face with Ria.

'I'll leave you,' Lulu said softly and withdrew.

Ria's eyes registered her concern. He didn't look well. He was not used to spending the night out in the open.

'Jimmy,' she said and she rushed forward to nuzzle her nose in his neck.

'You know that I have to leave?'

'Yes,' she said against his coat. 'But where will you go?'

'I'll be all right,' he said, 'now that I've seen you.'

She pulled back to look him in the eyes. 'I could come with you.'

He smiled sadly and shook his head. 'It wouldn't work,' he said. 'You can't go to the places I have to go. You have a pedigree, Ria. And a classy one at that. There would be people just waiting to snatch you and sell you to the highest bidder. I wouldn't be able to protect you and I can't let that happen.'

'But, Jimmy…'

He shook his head. 'It may seem a good idea now but, trust me, it wouldn't work.' He was quiet for a moment then he said, 'I just wanted to tell you that I… you know.'

Ria nodded. 'And I love you.'

He kissed the golden brown spot on her forehead, the mark of distinction that all Blenheims carry. And they stood close together, knowing they would probably never see each other again.

The voice of Lulu's mistress broke the spell. 'Lulu!' she called from her kitchen door. 'Come on. We're going out.'

'Why does it have to be like this?' Ria asked, her voice quavering. 'It's not fair. It's all happening so fast.'

Jimmy raised a paw, lifted her chin and smiled down at her.

'We'll always have Parish,' he said.

She nodded, tried to smile.

'See you, Ria,' he said and he backed away and was gone.

Paddy shook off the knotted football scarf and looped it over Jimmy's head. 'Once we get with the football crowd we'll be all right,' he said. 'The road is the quickest way, so it is, but it's too busy. An' we could be spotted by someone who knows us. Safest way is along the coast. There's quite a climb to get back up to the road but it's worth it.'

'Right,' Jimmy said, shaking the scarf into place.

They set off across Spring Meadow, a wide stretch of green that was less well tended than Parish Field and filled now with daisies and buttercups and dandelions. They were heading for the path that ran alongside the sand dunes, a path that was pitted with puddles from the recent rain.

'Was it okay back there?' Paddy asked.

'Yeah,' Jimmy said, but it was clear he didn't want to talk so Paddy left it and they trotted on in silence.

There was no one about until they had to pass two boys who were fishing from a river bank nearby. The boys saw Jimmy's scarf and immediately laughed and clapped their hands nine times in the salute football supporters give their team. To their surprise and delight Paddy barked twice in return.

Back on the road men and women, boys and girls converged on the railway station. The crowd seemed to be in great good humour and several people pointed out Jimmy's black and white scarf and cheered.

One man who spilled from a taxi in the station car park with a group of others bent down to pat him and ask, 'Howay, man, are you gannin' to the match?'

'Follow me,' Paddy said, leading Jimmy away from the queue at the ticket office, under a fence and on to the platform. The football special was already in. People were climbing aboard and the swell of passengers increased dramatically as a large party of supporters, wearing their black and white scarves, emerged from a coach.

'Stick with this lot,' Paddy advised, 'and you'll be all right.'

They faced each other now and Paddy said quietly, 'I'm so sorry you have to go, Jim lad. I'm not sure that waste of space Spence was worth all this.' And with a fond dog-style hug, he added, 'We'll really miss you, so we will. Goodbye now and good luck.'

Jimmy nodded and raised a paw as Paddy left to dodge under the fence and get back to the road. There was a moment now as he stood alone, surrounded by dozens of football fans and a little bewildered, when Jimmy caught his breath.

He had come almost face to face with Arthur, his owner. Arthur recognised him at once and it was as if he knew that this was Jimmy's means of escape. He didn't say anything. He simply smiled as if to say, 'I know you're a good dog, Jimmy, and I understand, too, that you have to go.'

Arthur noted the black and white scarf with an amused nod, held Jimmy's gaze fondly for a moment then winked his eye conspiratorially and boarded the train.

Alone again, wondering what the future might hold, Jimmy joined the cheerful, noisy, scarf-wearing football fans and boarded the train further down.

CHAPTER ELEVEN

A red sun spread across the early evening sky, like the broken yolk of a fried egg, as it slowly sank below the horizon. Already a pale moon hovered high, awaiting its turn to shine. The many day trippers had gone, the shops were closed and all was quiet in the village. And the Dogfather was not happy.

Don Schnauzer and The Professor were sitting in silence on the edge of the village green. The Professor was quiet because he knew something was wrong, something was bothering The Don and making him morose. No doubt Don Schnauzer would tell him what it was when he was ready.

Across the green Ali unlocked the door of his shop to let Rhavi out and Rhavi settled in the doorway to gaze at the sunset. But then he saw his friends and strolled across the road to join them.

'You don't look very happy,' he commented cheerfully, but there was no response. 'I mean, we lost Jimmy, yes. But we did save those poor little pups.'

Charlie Spence's van went by. He was out on bail, awaiting his trial. This was not his first offence and he knew he was facing a prison sentence. He was hoping to sell up before he went down and get out of the village where nobody liked him and he was clearly unwelcome. But nobody wanted his dilapidated bungalow or his neglected smallholding and planning permission for new buildings was very difficult to obtain. No one would deal with him anyway, not the local estate agent, not even the village store where Ali refused to serve him and he had to go into Bramble to buy his groceries.

'And we did get rid of the evil Spence,' The Professor added. 'It wasn't a bad result.'

'How can you say that?' Don Schnauzer asked. 'After what we've done to Jimmy.'

'Jimmy's young and strong,' The Professor said. 'He's intelligent, too. Some family will take him in, I'm sure. He's a fine dog.'

'That may be,' The Don said, 'but I believe we should do more, if only in honour of Jimmy. We owe it to him. Spence is only small fry, a nothing. I'm afraid what he was doing goes on every day all over the world. Dogs are being badly treated, made to hate each other, starved into fighting for scraps of food, abused by people who are not fit to be their owners. Getting rid of Spence won't change that.'

The Professor didn't say anything. He could see that the usually calm Don Schnauzer was consumed with anger.

'We got him out of the village,' Rhavi said. 'That's the main thing.'

'But it's not,' The Don said. 'It's not the main thing. We need to do much more than that.'

The Professor had known Don Schnauzer a long time and he knew, too, that once The Don set his sights on something not much could deter him.

'You have something in mind,' he said and it was not a question. It was a statement of fact.

'I've been thinking,' The Don said. 'You know that thing you are always telling us about? On the Internet. Place book or something.'

'Facebook,' The Professor said. 'Yes? What about it?'

'Well, from what you say, it's a simple way of contacting people all over the world. The United States, Canada, South America, Australia, Asia, Russia, Europe, anywhere in fact.'

The Professor nodded, frowning, not sure where this was leading.

'Well, suppose,' The Don said thoughtfully, 'suppose we send out a message to dogs everywhere, a request, no, a heartfelt plea.'

Rhavi's mouth fell open. 'Saying what, boss?'

'An appeal to dogs right across the world. Sniff out any illegal dog breeding, any organised dogfighting in your vicinity and expose it. Publish the names of all those people you suspect on the Internet and let the police investigate. Gather as much evidence as you possibly can and tell the world who these people are and what they're up to. Make it so obvious that police forces everywhere simply *have* to take action.'

'Dogs don't use the Internet,' The Professor said.

'You do,' The Don said, 'and unless I'm very much mistaken you're a dog. You don't think you'll be the only one, do you? There'll be dogs all over the world doing what you do. And anyway, we won't be just appealing to dogs. We want to get dog*lovers* involved. You can send out messages and no one will know you're a dog. And it's irrelevant anyway. We want to start a worldwide campaign against these people and we don't care how we do it. What about you, Rhavi? Can you use the Internet?'

'Never get a chance,' Rhavi said. 'If Ali goes out the missus stays in and vice versa.'

'I use mine at night,' The Professor said.

'Yeah, well,' Rhavi said. 'Ours is upstairs. In *their* bedroom. It would look a bit odd if they woke up and found me tapping away on Facebook.'

'We'll have a meeting to discuss this,' Don Schnauzer said. 'We'll get all the gang together. See what we can come up with.'

'That Lulu reckons she's on Facebook,' Rhavi said. 'She says she has a boyfriend in Australia and another in LA.'

The Professor looked at Don Schnauzer knowingly. 'You're serious about this, aren't you?'

The Dogfather nodded soberly. 'Absolutely, Professor.'

And so it was that a series of forceful messages appeared on the Internet across the world. The Professor contacted all the many friends he had made on Facebook, put out the message and asked them to pass it on to all *their* friends, as people do in one of those chain letters.

The message spread like a forest fire. Within days support from many quarters was quick to emerge, gaining momentum and taking off, and within weeks the message had become a major news item.

Doglovers everywhere were taking up the cause and demanding action against anyone, anywhere, suspected of taking part in or supporting what a well-known television commentator called 'this odious cruelty'. There may well have been a great many dogs spreading the message, like The Professor, via the Internet, but nobody knew who was a dog or who wasn't. And it didn't matter, anyway, as long as the message got through.

Newspapers, eager not to miss out on this eye-catching new phenomenon, carried banner headlines: FLUSH OUT THESE EVIL PEOPLE and DOGFIGHT DEALERS WE KNOW WHO YOU ARE. One newspaper gave out lapel badges to children or anyone who wanted to wear one. The badges showed the face of a sad and badly injured pit bull terrier encircled by the words: 'Fight to stop these fights!' And soon the badges were in great demand.

It was not long before the names and addresses of suspected breeders and fight organisers began to appear in abundance on websites across the world. The views were sought of animal-loving celebrities, television pundits held discussions and the police forces of many countries were forced to react. There were, of course, many unfair and false accusations but ninety per cent or more were genuine. Most of the accused were taken into custody and charged, others simply disappeared.

Nightly on television now there were shots of aggressive and cruel looking men and women being rounded up and hustled into police vans. In the UK the campaign figured daily in BBC and ITV newscasts and in news bulletins in many countries.

CNN, Bloomberg, Euronews, Sky News, France 24, Al Jazeera, Russia Today, in fact, every major broadcaster carried the story. So strong was the public response that questions were asked in the House of Commons and the Prime Minister saw fit to make a statement promising the courts would 'come down heavily' on anyone engaging in these illegal and abhorrent activities.

One Member of Parliament tabled a motion to tighten up the law, proposing that all owners and prospective owners of pit bull terriers must submit to a stricter 'test of suitability'. In other words, to check that they were intelligent and genuine doglovers and not the backward, sad and inadequate individuals who use their dogs as weapons or, worse still, are intent on training them to fight in secret contests hidden away in remote barns and backwaters.

Ringo barked three times, waited then barked again and soon the gang assembled in the copse.

The Professor held up a paw. 'Silence, please. Our Dogfather.'

Respectfully the gang fell silent as Don Schnauzer stood before them. 'Brothers,' he began quietly in his muffled voice, 'I believe we can now rejoice in the sure knowledge that our campaign to name and shame those individuals and gangs who, for their own mindless entertainment and profit, force our fellow dogs to fight each other, has been an unqualified success.

'Many of these undesirables, who are unfit to call themselves human beings, have been rounded up and put into prisons where they belong, where they can no longer harm any of our brethren.'

Don Schnauzer was smiling and a great cheer of barking went

on until The Professor again held up a paw.

'It is my wish,' Don Schnauzer announced, 'that the success of this campaign be dedicated to our dear friend Jimmy.'

The Professor, Max, Paddy, Rhavi, Ringo and Chalkie all stood at once and raised a paw in a respectful response.

'To Jimmy,' they declared.

'We all played a part in this enterprise,' The Don went on. 'Not least the Rottweilers, Rocky and Rambo, who acquitted themselves brilliantly. Now, thanks to Max, they have promising careers ahead of them. Thank you, Max.'

Max lay down and stretched out, a little embarrassed. 'Ah, it was nothing,' he said. 'They were good lads. They deserved a break.'

'And Paddy's brilliant idea to smuggle Jimmy aboard the football train was a master stroke,' The Don added.

'It was clever, so it was,' Paddy agreed, congratulating himself, his chest puffed out. 'A brilliant idea, though I say it meself.'

'Rhavi, Ringo, Chalkie, you all played your part,' The Don told them, 'and, of course, we must congratulate The Professor whose exceptional IT skills and technical know-how enabled us to mount our worldwide attack on the forces of evil. Thank you, Professor, and thank you all, thank you very much indeed. Congratulations to you all.'

He paused then went on quietly, 'The problem in the beginning was how to gain the confidence and the co-operation of Spence's guard dogs. This was essential if we were to have any hope of success. We must not forget that Jimmy did that to perfection.'

Don Schnauzer paused again then said, with a heavy heart, 'It is the one regret I have about all this that we have lost him. We all loved Jimmy and we will not forget him. It is my hope and my dearest wish that he will find a good home with people who will love him and take care of him.'

‘Hear! Hear!’ sounded round the copse.

Chalkie covered his eyes with his paws, trying but failing to hide his grief. ‘It’s all my fault,’ he sobbed.

But Rhavi said, ‘Jimmy didn’t bear you any grudge, Chalkie. He simply did what he had to do.’

‘It’s not fair,’ Chalkie wailed. ‘He’s not a dangerous dog.’

‘Jimmy would have come to the rescue of any one of us in trouble,’ The Don told him. ‘You must not blame yourself.’

Paddy was holding up a paw.

‘Yes, Paddy,’ The Don said.

‘Dogfather,’ Paddy began, ‘I think it would be only fair for us to send a message to the bitches, Ria and my good friend Lulu. After all, it was they who brought Spence’s activities to our attention, so it was.’

‘Quite right, Paddy,’ The Don agreed. ‘And we will leave that in your capable paws. You must give the bitches our very best wishes and thank them on behalf of us all for the very important part they played.’

Paddy’s tail wagged wildly. ‘I’ll do that, so I will,’ he said.

Don Schnauzer nodded at The Professor and The Professor held up a paw. ‘And so I declare this meeting closed,’ he said.

The gang dispersed, satisfied with a job well done, and as they walked back, side by side, to the village, the Dogfather turned again to The Professor. ‘You know, Prof,’ he said, ‘so often, when things are not right, all it takes is for the underdog to make a stand and fight back.’

CHAPTER TWELVE

But that's not the end of the story. Not quite. The Dogfather, The Professor, Chalkie and all the gang were desperately sad about what happened to Jimmy. But the way things turned out, Jimmy was all right in the end.

He was on the train with all the football fans and the fans were laughing and shouting, singing their team's songs and, as always, thoroughly enjoying the occasion. It was what they looked forward to all week. Jimmy's eyes were bright and shining and his tail was wagging wildly but he was not happy. He was only pretending to enjoy the party. He wanted to get to the city now and find his way around, find somewhere to stay for a while.

It was all right for the football-mad fans. They would see the match and, win or lose, they would have their homes and their beds to go to. Jimmy had to find some place where tonight he could lay his head in safety and he wanted to do that before it grew dark.

The 'Soccer Special' sped along, racing by small wayside stations until there were fewer fields and more and more buildings. Then the two lines of track branched out and there were several tracks as the train slowed down to approach the main station. Clanking over the points as the end of a platform went gliding by, the train eased itself with a hissing sound, like a sigh of relief, to a standstill. A porter with a small green flag was waiting.

As the fans stood up and formed an orderly queue to leave the train, Jimmy drew himself in between two back-to-back seats. The carriage doors opened and the scarf-wearing fans spilled out on to the platform and moved along like a black and white incoming tide.

Jimmy waited, then he shook off the scarf. He was anxious to get away from the crowd and explore the city. The carriage had soon emptied and was suddenly, strangely quiet. He hurried off, not wanting to be locked in.

A porter looked at him in surprise, expecting to see his owner follow him off, but Jimmy panicked and ran away fast. There was a high footbridge and he climbed the metal steps rapidly to cross to the opposite platform. But as he came down to the other side another railman was looking up at him, waiting and clearly hoping to catch him. Jimmy turned abruptly, ran back the way he came and down to the platform he arrived at.

The two railmen were calling to each other across the tracks and he knew they were talking about him. A stray dog running about the station! It was a very dangerous situation and it was their job to deal with it. Jimmy realised his best way of escape would be to rejoin the football crowd, at least until he was out on the street.

He sprinted to join the end of the crowd that was moving ahead slowly in a narrowing crush and then suddenly the congestion eased and he found he was in the main hall. Dodging between moving legs he sought a way through and soon he could see a clear patch of sky. He was almost out to the street but as he emerged into a relatively clear patch he saw a small boy with a tear-stained face.

The boy was aged about five and he was clearly feeling sorry for himself. Jimmy stopped in his tracks and, forgetting for the moment that the railmen were after him, he turned and came back. He looked at the boy closely and saw that he was crying, his face crumpled and his pink cheeks smudged where he had tried to brush away his tears.

Jimmy put his head down and gently, affectionately, he nuzzled the boy's midriff. He wanted to comfort him, tell him there was no need to cry. If he was lost he would soon be found. He looked deep into the little boy's eyes, wishing there was a way he could convey all this, his own problems forgotten for now.

The boy's lower lip came out but he stopped crying and, looking at Jimmy, he seemed to respond. Jimmy crouched low beside him, and instinctively the boy stroked his head.

Jimmy's presence seemed to calm and comfort the boy now as they sat down, side by side, in the huge hall, and the boy's arm went around Jimmy's neck. It was as if he felt as long as Jimmy was there, he was safe.

What was left of the football supporters slowly passed through the main exit and the hall gradually became less congested. One or two passers-by glanced their way but the little boy no longer seemed a cause for concern. His tears had given way to the occasional cross between a sob and a hiccup but, with Jimmy by his side, he seemed much more composed.

A large man came running then stopped, his face drained and anxious as he looked around. He was panic stricken, then he saw the boy and his eyes lit up in delight and he ran forward.

'Freddie!' he cried and he picked up the little boy and swung him round. 'I thought I'd lost you, running off like that!'

He had turned away for a second to look at a rail timetable and Freddie had wandered off and was lost in the crowd.

Jimmy stood up slowly. The boy was safe now, clinging to his father's neck. All's well that ends well, Jimmy told himself. It was time to go. But the little boy suddenly said, 'Daddy, no!'

He struggled to be put down then, clinging tightly, his arms were around Jimmy's neck. The colour restored to his friendly face Freddie's father looked like an outdoor man, a farmer perhaps. He smiled down at Jimmy.

'Did this handsome fella take care of you, son?' he asked. He knelt on one knee and patted Jimmy gratefully. 'Thank you, pal. Thank you for taking care of my little man here.'

Slowly, his head still down, Jimmy began to back away. It was time to go, he told himself. Then he saw that one of the railmen who had chased him earlier was rapidly approaching.

'Sir,' the porter told the big man, 'we can't have dogs running loose around the station. A dog must be on a lead at all times. It's very dangerous otherwise. It could cause an accident. People could get hurt. Your dog could get hurt, especially if he ran on to the tracks.'

Jimmy wanted to make his escape, run for the exit, but the little boy, Freddie, had his arm locked securely around Jimmy's neck and he was simply refusing to let go.

'This is not my dog,' Freddie's father said mildly.

The porter looked puzzled. 'Not your dog?'

'No,' the big man said, noting that Jimmy was not wearing a collar, 'but his owner can't be far away. A fine dog like this.'

The porter looked around the wide hall. 'In that case, sir,' he said, 'if the owner can't be found he's a stray. I'm going to have to take him to the office, call up the Dog Warden.'

'And what happens then?' the big man asked.

'Well,' the porter said confidentially, not wanting the boy to hear, 'if the owner can't be found and they can't find a good home for him...' His voice trailed. 'So many strays these days they have to be, y'know.'

Freddie was tugging at his father's trouser leg, 'No, Daddy!' he wailed, his arm still around Jimmy's neck. 'He's *my* dog.'

'He's not your dog, Freddie,' his father said gently. 'He doesn't belong to us. His owner must be found.'

But the boy was not going to give Jimmy up without a fight. 'He can live with us. He's mine now. I want to keep him.'

The boy's father wavered. They lived on a farm and their own dog, Shep, was quite old now. Old Shep could do with some help around the place, he convinced himself. But really he was feeling guilty about losing his little boy in the crowd and he didn't want to upset him again.

'Well, look,' he said, ' We have plenty of room on the farm and we can take good care of him. We can give him a good home if necessary.' He handed the porter a printed card. 'Suppose we take him and if the owner comes forward you can give him my address?'

Jimmy listened, his eyes bright, his tail wagging. He loved the outdoors. He wanted to shout aloud, 'My dad was a sheep dog!'

The porter looked at the card: Fairholme Farm, Hexton Lane. He pushed his hat to the back of his head. 'Well, I suppose,' he said uncertainly, 'if you're sure.' He peered at the card again. 'We have your 'phone number and your e-mail address.'

Freddie was jumping up and down with excitement and Jimmy decided not to run away.

The big man shook hands with the porter and, with Freddie and Jimmy in tow, he led the way out to the car park and his station wagon. Jimmy and Freddie snuggled up close on the back seat, Freddie again with his arm around Jimmy.

Fairholme Farm was a lovely place with several acres of fields, and cows and sheep and even an old goat. Freddie had an older brother and sister and they all made a great fuss of Jimmy. But for all the love and affection they showered on him there was never any doubt that he was Freddie's dog and always would be.

It was soon after he arrived at the farm, when he was sitting watching television with Freddie, that the BBC news came on. Jimmy sat up and listened intently when the newsreader said people who were breeding pit bull terriers to engage in illegal dogfighting were being rounded up and arrested. Someone had posted a notice on Facebook aimed at doglovers everywhere, urging them to seek out and expose these people. Apparently the message had been taken up by other chat lines and was spreading worldwide.

The campaign, the newsreader said, had been a remarkable success and was still gaining momentum. Nobody knew, he added, who had started it. Jimmy smiled to himself, convinced it was The Professor and the rest of the gang.

Of course nobody came to claim Jimmy and he lived a long, contented, outdoor life with Freddie and the family. He was as happy as could be, though he did, now and then, remember a long lazy afternoon on the Parish field, and, of course, he thought of Ria.

THE END